# THE COMPLETE CASES OF
# THE BLUE BARREL, VOLUME I

WILLIAM E. BARRETT

# THE COMPLETE CASES OF THE

# BLUE BARREL™

## VOLUME 1

# WILLIAM E. BARRETT

PRIMARY ILLUSTRATOR

## JOHN FLEMING GOULD

STEEGER BOOKS • 2019

PUBLISHING HISTORY

"Dead Man's Choice" originally appeared in the November 1933 issue of *Strange Detective Stories* magazine. Copyright 1933 by Nickel Publications Inc.

"The Mobster Man" originally appeared in the December 1933 issue of *Strange Detective Stories* magazine. Copyright 1933 by Nickel Publications Inc.

"The Blue Barrel" originally appeared in the March 1936 issue of *Dime Detective* magazine. Copyright 1936 by Popular Publications, Inc. Copyright renewed 1963 and assigned to Steeger Properties, LLC. All rights reserved.

"Death on the Double-O" originally appeared in the July 1936 issue of *Dime Detective* magazine. Copyright 1936 by Popular Publications, Inc. Copyright renewed 1963 and assigned to Steeger Properties, LLC. All rights reserved.

"A Man's Last Hours" originally appeared in the September 1936 issue of *Dime Detective* magazine. Copyright 1936 by Popular Publications, Inc. Copyright renewed 1963 and assigned to Steeger Properties, LLC. All rights reserved.

"Ring Around a Murder" originally appeared in the December 1936 issue of *Dime Detective* magazine. Copyright 1936 by Popular Publications, Inc. Copyright renewed 1963 and assigned to Steeger Properties, LLC. All rights reserved.

Thanks to Kevin Cook and Judy Lloyd.

# TABLE OF CONTENTS

# DEAD MAN'S CHOICE

HE DIED TWICE, AND WITH HIS
LAST GASP LEFT A LEGACY OF
FEAR THAT GREW TO WHIRLWIND
PROPORTIONS UNDER THE VERY
SHADOW OF THE CAPITOL DOME.

**D**EAN CULVER lighted his last cigarette with his last match and settled back comfortably on his park bench. There was a man lurking in the bushes within twenty feet of the bench and Culver was interested. The man was paying no attention to Culver; he was watching the apartment house across the street.

Lafayette Park was dimly lighted. By looking over his shoulder, Culver could see the White House with the floodlighted peak of the Washington Monument beyond it. Culver wasn't interested. He was new to Washington but he already had ideas about the monument. It was beautiful but it was also hard. And it was as smooth as the people who lived in its long shadow.

The man in the bushes shifted his position. He seemed nervous, impatient. Culver classified him easily. The man had none of the grim tautness of the stick-up or the lurking assassin. There was something impersonal about him.

"A dick. Tailing someone in the tony flop across the street."

Culver blew the smoke lazily through his nostrils. This wasn't Chicago, but it could be. Some of the props were familiar. Culver had learned his book well in the days when he was reporting police in the big city on the lake. He felt no urge to call a cop when he saw a man hiding in the

Dean had time to mumble only one word before the fellow swung.

bushes; he was willing to admit that the man might conceivably belong right where he was.

With a grunt, the watcher turned. Still keeping the apartment house under surveillance, the man crossed the path to Culver's bench. He was short, wiry and dressed inconspicuously. His eyes were sharp and they darted over Culver's lean length in quick appraisal.

"Want to make a quick buck, Buddy?" His voice was low pitched.

Culver rolled the cigarette along his lips. It was a laugh. The idea of some gumshoe picking him off a bench for flop money. The smoke trickled in thin streams from his nostrils. The loudest laugh was that he needed the dollar. He nodded his head.

"How do I make it?"

"Easy." The little man shot another quick glance at the apartment house. "I'm tailin' a guy in there. Silk hatter. He'll have a mugg with him. His car will roll up front. Probably Oklahoma pads. You delay the guy. Hit him for change or spin a weep. I don't care. Just delay him. I'll be back on the job in a minute."

He was holding out a limp dollar. Culver took it and rammed it in his pocket. "Okay, Brother," he said softly. "Consider the guy delayed."

**HE CROSSED** Eye Street in long strides while the little man made a bee line for the park comfort station, twenty-five feet off the corner. Culver's lips twitched.

Being stooge for a shadow was hardly a career; but it was a job. He eyed the apartment house.

Flush with "H" Street on the one side, it set back comfortably from Sixteenth Street in front with a private driveway. Bending backward with dignity, it carried its name on a plate too small to be read from the street. Sixteenth Street, itself, was all but deserted, but there was a solitary car of expensive make waiting for the green light at Eye Street. Culver hummed softly.

If that car was calling for the silk hatter, he would be down in a few seconds. A man who did any delaying would not do it out here on the sidewalk. He stalked up the sidewalk toward the apartment front. The car passed him on the driveway before he reached the entrance. It had Oklahoma plates.

"Just a minute, Mister."

Culver hurried forward as the tall gray haired man swept majestically through the lackey-held doors. The man hesitated, his foot on the running board. He had broad features and a grim jaw. His eyes were narrowed.

"Could you spare a—" Culver wasn't well up in his lines and they came hard. A broad shouldered man who wore evening clothes like a hula dancer would wear a driver's outfit, stepped forward.

"Okay, boss," he said gruffly. His fist zoomed from the vicinity of his waist and Culver saw it coming too late. The lights seemed to dance and shimmy, the pavement spun under his feet and there was a lot of noise. The ground came up to him.

The knockout was only momentarily. It might have lasted through a ten count, but it wouldn't have kept the man from Chi on the ground for fourteen. He blinked and rolled over on the grass just as the big car whipped around the corner on H. Groggily, he regained his feet and shook his head. He was alone on the grass and the apartment front was as quiet and as dignified as when he first saw it. The broad-shouldered boy with the fist had worked so smoothly that the lad holding the door inside had seen nothing to lure him out of doors.

"Well, I earned that buck even if I am one rotten delayer."

With a tug at his hat brim and an impatient shake of his shoulders, Culver retraced his way. There was no sign of the little man who had been keeping vigil in the bushes. An old and very inconspicuous car of a fast make was standing against the H Street curb on the Lafayette Park side. Culver had an idea that it belonged to the shadow. He passed it and looked inside; then he turned toward the comfort station. Cutting at right angles to the path and pushing the bushes out of his way, he stumbled over something limp on the grass. He stopped dead with his foot half raised; then he set it down on the grass again and bent over.

The man who had lurked in the bushes was lying under them now. His body sprawled in a curiously limp, spread-eagle fashion.

Culver cursed softly and fumbled for a match. He remembered then that he had used his last match. Bending low, he fumbled in the pockets of the man on the ground. A container of paper matches rewarded his search and he lighted one, shielding it with his hand.

**THE SHADOW** lay on his back with his mouth open and with his chest dyed red. There were tiny bubbles on his lips but he was not quite dead. His eyes moved when he felt the light, but they were glassy eyes. Culver crouched over him.

"Lake—Lake—Mack Agency—" The man's voice was a thin, tortured whisper. Culver wet his lips.

"Okay, Bud. Who got you?"

The man tried to move, to lift his head. His face seemed to turn to wax with the effort and his chest erupted the red fluid that was his life. He relaxed like a deflated balloon and Culver was not guessing when he dropped the second match and turned away from the body. He had seen them die before and he did not need a medical certificate of cause.

Somebody had been silently stalking the little man even as he stood watch over the apartment house across the way. In the short time that it had taken Culver to cross the street and take his punch on the chin, the stalker had struck with murderous efficiency. The victim had had little chance for an outcry or a struggle.

"Swell place for me to be."

Culver looked around cautiously. It was quiet in this corner of the park and there was no traffic on H Street except for an occasional auto speeding past. It was too late for many pedestrians to be out, but there was bound to be a few. And there would be a Cop on the beat.

"Open and shut for the local boys if I hang around." Culver pulled his hat brim down. "I'm it. Well, when I take a rap, I'll know more about it than I know about this one."

He turned into the deeper shadows of the Park away from H Street and walked in the direction of the White House and Pennsylvania Avenue. He felt no compunction about leaving the body behind him. There was nothing that could be done for the man now and Culver was not good at explanations. He had heard that the Washington cops were a bunch of cossacks and he wasn't anxious for proof.

He had seen crimes solved before by master-minders who deducted best with a piece of rubber hose or a sapper.

There was a big hotel on Fourteenth Street and Culver consulted a phone book. The Mack Agency, he found, was in a building up on G Street. He whistled softly and went out.

"Somebody might be on the job. It's worth a try."

He swung toward G Street, his lips grim. Less than an hour ago, he had been broke and out of a job. Now he had a dollar and he knew where there was a vacancy. Some people might be squeamish about the idea of going after a man's job while the man was still lying in his own blood. Culver didn't react that way. He had been sucked into a deal, he'd taken a poke on the chin and he'd seen a man die. He wanted to draw cards and stay in the game.

The white fronted building on G Street was open and there was a colored boy reading a magazine in the lobby. Culver gave the directory board a quick once-over and moved toward the elevator. The Mack Agency was 802.

"I ain't supposed to take you up, boss, less'n you're a tenant."

The boy fumbled his magazine doubtfully. Culver grunted.

"Mack's expecting me. Shake it up...."

"Oh. Mister Mack. Yessir." The boy got in and slapped the door closed. The elevator started up and Culver smiled grimly. Washington or Chi, private agencies were all alike; they kept their own hours and made their own rules.

If that were not true, he'd be a rube to walk in with the story that he had to tell. Regular dicks are prejudiced against people who walk away from murders.

# CHAPTER TWO
## I'M YOUR MAN

**T**HE DOOR of 802 was unlocked. There was a reception hall with a deserted telephone switchboard facing the door. A low hum of voices came from the private office behind the board. The door was closed but light gleamed through the glass. As the outside door clicked behind Culver, the conversation stopped. Culver took a quick stride and opened the door. A lean, chalk-faced man came half-way to his feet; one hand in his pocket. Culver waved him down.

"No guns, soldier. This is a peace parley...."

He shifted his glance to the other man who hadn't stirred. He was looking into a broad, moon-shaped face liberally dewed with perspiration. He nodded.

"You, Mack?"

"Sure. What can I do for you?"

The big man waved the chalk-faced one back to a chair with one pudgy hand. There was a genial smile on his face but his eyes did not seem to cooperate heartily with his lips. They were small eyes set far apart and almost completely hidden behind bunkers of flesh. A black lettered sign dominated the wall at the man's back. "THINK NOTHING OF IT."

"I came up for a job." Culver pulled a chair over and flopped into it. The pale-faced man was watching him narrowly. He had very dark eyes, thin lips and a long, bony jaw. Mack rolled a cigar on his lips without lighting it.

"It's two A.M.," he said. "Shoot clean, fella. What do you want?"

"Just that. A job. One of your men just got himself bumped. I want to carry on."

The cigar did a fast roll across the fat lips and the big man tensed. Chalk-face leaned forward. Culver leaned back. He knew when he had the other fellow coming in. It was no time to lead. Mack laid his hand flat on the desk.

"How do you know he was killed?"

"I found him."

Mack looked at Culver quietly. That broad, fat face told nothing. It still looked genial. "How'd you know he belonged here?"

It was a logical question, but the logical answer is not always the right one. Culver smelled a sour note in the symphony and the papers had taught him to absorb information without imparting it. He wondered why there was no surprise shown at the mention of murder. If the cops had found the body and notified Mack, why was he hanging around his office? Culver shrugged.

"The guy gave me a buck to watch an apartment house for him a few minutes. He told me he was Mack Agency. He didn't come back. I found him conked."

"Humph." Mack looked over at the chalk-faced man, who had relaxed somewhat. The man nodded his head; then, as though he were afraid that Culver would draw any false conclusions from the nod, he leaned forward.

"The story sounds straight," he said. "Did he tell you his name?"

Culver raised his brows. "Why should he? All I wanted to know was whether I was watching a spot for a hood or teaming with a guy that had business on the legit."

"Did you go through him?" Mack was taking care of the conversation again. Culver laughed.

"I never touched him. I should leave prints or something for the dicks. I'm a stranger in town."

The big man breathed softly. "You know your way," he said. "We can use you." He looked over at the chalk-faced man again; then his lips smiled and hurled the lie at his eyes once more.

"It's like this," he said. "The cop's name was Carr. He was working out of here on a case that's pretty big. Did you read about that Oklahoma Indian that got bumped a few nights ago?"

Culver shook his head. "I'm a stranger here." His eyes were narrowed. He was interested in learning that the murdered man's name was Carr. He hadn't suspected that. It gave a different value to the man's dying statement. Mack leaned back and lighted his cigar.

"The Injun's name was Mike Wendell. He was filthy with jack. One of those Oklahoma Osages Oil. He came up here to raise hell with the Indian bureau. Had an idea that the noble redman was being rooked by the black gold boys."

THE CIGAR did a quick round trip over the broad lip. The party was all very pleasant now. Even Chalk-face seemed comfortable. He was leaning back. Mack's voice was conversational.

"Our client was Richard Richards, the bird they call Double Dick. He's an oil lobbyist and smart. This Injun didn't worry him any, but he wanted to know who the Injun was seeing and who was listening to his gripe. That was our job; tailing the Injun."

He shrugged and made an expansive gesture. "That was okay until the Injun calls on Double Dick for a private pow wow. Right after that, Mr. Richards calls us off and—" He leaned forward and the smoke came slowly from his nostrils. "The first night we aren't tailin' him, the Injun gets rubbed out."

He raised his pale eyebrows and held them suspended while he stared at Culver, his lips pursed. The effect would be comical if the implication of the words was less grim. Culver balanced his chair on the two rear legs.

"So what? You think your client had the Injun smoked?"

Mack looked pained. "I never jump at conclusions in my business. I ain't supposed to. But an agency has a rep to maintain. At my own expense, I've been keeping track o' this Double Dick." He spread his hands wide. "Tonight, Carr is watching him and he gets rubbed out while he's doing it. What would you think?"

"I wouldn't. I don't jump at conclusions, either."

Culver reached over and took a cigarette from the chalk-faced man's package. He was thinking hard. It was a good story and a lot of it clicked. The man who had entered the car with the Oklahoma pads had not been an Indian; he was the type who might be a lobbyist. The murdered dick had been watching him. Culver lighted up.

"Has this Double Dick got a slugger that travels with him?"

Mack tensed. "He has. Feller named Tub Casson. Why?"

"I just owe him a rap in the jaw. That's why. But say on. Where do I fit the picture? What's my job?"

The big man beamed at him, but the beaming expression seemed to be frozen on the man's face—a mask thrown up hastily as a cover while a shrewd brain worked furiously. Culver waited. More than ever, he felt that he was walking into something big, something more than half hidden; a game where men were contending at cross purposes and where death was only incidental to the stakes.

Mack grunted suddenly and the frozen geniality warmed. "Before I can give you a job out of this agency," he said slowly, "I've got to enroll you as an op. Can't turn you loose as a Mack man without protection."

He bit had on the cigar. "Guess you can't get a bond right away. I'll waive that. I got to get a form filled, though and—" he paused. "I've got to get a reference from some agency where you worked."

"No good. I never worked at an agency. Newspapers but no agencies."

"Humph!" The big man looked sharply at the chalk-faced one; then he smiled with relief. "We can fix that," he said. "I just happened to remember. Lake, here, has a brother with an agency in Baltimore. Got some blank letter-heads, Phil?"

"Yeah." The white-faced man crossed to a desk in the corner. Culver inhaled thoughtfully, his eyes hooded. So this man's name was Lake. And the murdered man's name was Carr. Nice little set-up.

Lake was banging on the typewriter. He was only a few minutes at the machine. The result of his labors was a curt note on the letter-head of a Baltimore detective agency.

> To whom it may concern:
> Dean Culver is well known to this agency as a skilled and reliable operative. He is discreet and of sober habits.
> Lester Wade, Mgr.

Culver did not change expression. He had given his right name, but he noticed that, if the agency was managed by Lake's brother, the signature was not that of anyone named "Lake." The big man was shoving a form across the desk to him.

"Just fill this out. Name, last address, a few references, etc. Under that references, you can just write, 'See attached.'"

"Sure." Culver did not raise his head. The Mack Agency rolled smoothly. He filled in the blanks and slid the paper across the desk. "How about a rod and an advance?"

"A rod?" Mack shook his head. "Can't do it. You'd have to have a license, son. And advance?" He pursed his lips. "I'll let you have twenty."

"Okay." Culver stood up. "Now I want some clippings on that Injun kill and my first assignment."

The big man hesitated, then he spun around in his chair, flipped a clipping out of the file; tossed a crumpled twenty-dollar bill after it.

"Your first job," he said cheerfully, "is to drop down to H.Q. and see if the cops have anything on the Carr kill that they don't want to spill over the phone. After that, come back."

Culver headed for the door. "Okay," he said softly. "Thanks."

The big man beamed at him. "Think nothing of it," he said.

## CHAPTER THREE

## DOLLAR DOWN DEATH

"**G**O DOWN to Police H.Q. and ask some questions about the bump; then come back. That's a laugh."

Culver whistled softly under his breath as he stepped out on G Street. He had a life-size picture of the cops telling all to an unknown private dick. He had a more convincing conception of the cops falling on his neck with a few questions of their own. He had a picture, too, that wasn't so convincing of the bland Mr. Mack backing him up. He shook his head.

"Nice little headline," he said. "Chicago boy gets taken for an airing in D.C. Well, maybe—"

He crossed G Street. There were a few cruising hacks and he flagged one. "Go up the block half way and wait there facing this way," he said. "When I give you the high sign, roll down here. Sabe?"

"Do I do it for love or something?" The hacker was look-ing at him suspiciously. Culver grinned and passed him the crumpled dollar.

"You do it for a dollar down and more when you catch me, Bozo. Roll it."

He was watching the building across the way. He didn't know if he'd need the hack, but if he did need it, he'd need it fast, and he wanted it where he could get it.

There was a ladies' wear store at his back with an arcade type front. He stepped back into the arcade and took his stand behind the center window. He could see the build-ing entrance across the way through the glass, but he was not conspicuous himself. While he waited, he read the clipping.

There was little about the Indian murder that he hadn't been told. Mike Wendell, an Osage Indian, had come up to Washington with a petition to the Indian Bureau. He had been last seen alive by the doorman of his hotel when he left early in the evening, crossed the street and got into an expensive sedan. The doorman did not notice the make, the license plates or the occupants. Next morning, the Indian's body had been found in a culvert over the Mary-land line. He had been shot twice and robbed. According to Jimmy Troll, a Montana Indian who had been friendly with him, Wendell had been accustomed to carrying as much as ten thousand dollars in his pockets. He also wore an expensive diamond ring. He was addicted to gambling and the police had a theory that he had fallen into the hands of crooked gamblers or that he had aroused the cupidity of gangsters by a display of wealth in some gambling house. There were no clues.

Culver folded the clipping away thoughtfully. There seemed to be more than one motive for the Indian's murder. The Carr case was different. If the two were linked, it narrowed the search. Incidentally, it made things look a bit dark for the unknown Double Dick, lobbyist. He might, conceivably, have something at stake that would make the ten thousand cash look like chicken feed.

The door of the white building opened and Culver tensed. Mack and Phil Lake stepped out, looked carefully up and down G Street; then walked toward the corner. The big man was chuckling, but the other walked like a phantom; tall, grim, loose jointed; a cigarette stuck against his lower lip and dangling. At the corner they paused for a moment; then headed for a parked sedan. Culver stepped half way out of his hiding place and held up two fingers. The hack rolled slowly down G Street.

The sedan was pointed out Fourteenth. It snorted and came to life. As it flashed away, the hack pulled up in front of the ladies' wear store and Culver jumped in. "Stay with 'em, buddy." They snorted away and turned into Fourteenth fast.

The sedan was already two blocks away but the hack opened up. It was only a block behind when they turned left on K and the rest was easy. The driver of the sedan was obviously not aware of pursuit, nor was he suspicious. He pulled to the curb a few feet away from the entrance of a small hotel on Seventeenth. Culver flagged his hack down at the corner. Mack and Lake got out.

The Agency manager crossed the street to an all night restaurant. Lake fumbled with the brim of his hat and, cigarette still dangling, entered the hotel. Culver's eyes gleamed with excitement.

"Okay, Buddy. You're through."

**HE PAID** the driver and swung for the alley on foot. Coming up behind the hotel, he discovered an areaway from which he could look across the street. Mack was sitting on the corner stool at the beanery counter across the way. He was watching the hotel and, of course, there would be a wall phone in the beanery. Neat.

Culver retraced his way and went in through the back of the hotel. A colored man in overalls looked at him curiously, but did not challenge him. It was a break. The service stairs opened on a little hall that paralleled the lounge. Culver stepped into the lounge and crossed to a wall desk. There was only a dim light burning. He took some stationery from the desk and wrote a short, meaningless note. He addressed it to "Mr. Carr," sealed the envelope and walked out into the lobby. A sleepy looking desk clerk looked up as he approached. Culver played it safe. After all, he could be wrong.

"I want to leave a note for Mr. Lake."

The clerk shook his head. "We have no Mr. Lake registered."

Culver snapped his fingers. "Did I say Lake? My mistake." He slid the envelope across the desk. "I meant Mr. Carr."

The clerk looked down at the envelope. "Ah, yes." He reached languidly behind him and flipped the envelope into a box. Culver's eyes followed the envelope and he made a note of the number. He waved his thanks and turned back into the lounge. The clerk seemed uninterested. Culver smiled, then his mouth tightened.

"The lad evidently hasn't heard what happened to the tenant of 406," he said softly. "I wonder if anybody has found him yet?"

He went back to the service stairs and ascended softly to the fourth floor. His brow was wrinkled and he was wondering, as he had wondered many times before, just who Carr was. He wondered, too, why Mack and Lake hadn't come up sooner as long as they were coming. It was a cinch that the cops would be along pretty fast after the body was found and identified. Why take a chance on being around when they came; and why come at all?

He shrugged and moved silently along the carpeted hallway of the fourth floor. There was a thin line of light under 406. His hand moved instinctively to where his shoulder holster would be if he were wearing a shoulder holster. He cursed softly as he withdrew the hand empty. His fist clenched and he looked at it; then, with no more pretense of quiet, he walked to 406 and knocked at the door.

The sound of faint movement within the room ceased. Culver knocked again. He pitched his voice high. "Special delivery for you, Mr. Carr."

Someone crossed the room and stopped on the other side of the door. "Slip it under the door."

"Can't do it, Mr. Carr. It's registered. You gotta sign."

That was curiosity bait and Culver could fairly feel the indecision within the room. Then the knob turned softly and he gathered himself. As the door opened a crack, Culver threw his left like a fighter who jabs an opponent off balance. The flat of his hand came against the door and it opened. Culver's right followed the left and boomed into the aperture....

He had a vision of a chalk white face as the blow went home; then he was jumping after the punch. Sprawling backward with his hands clutching wide, Lake was a beautiful target and Culver nailed him twice; then, as the man started to the floor, Culver caught him and spun him into the bed. His hand dipped inside the other's coat and came out with a flat, ugly automatic. He laughed softly. Lake struggled to get up, his eyes wide.

"You— You— What are you doing here?"

"I needed a gun, Bozo, and you guys wouldn't give me one."

**CULVER'S EYES** swept the room. There was a sheaf of slips on a wall desk beside a battered portable typewriter. The room had the appearance of having been thoroughly searched. Lake was holding his bony jaw and glaring.

"You made a bull, pulling an act like this. You can't get away with it. You—"

"I am getting away with it." Culver shook the automatic suggestively. "You flop in that big chair over there and be nice."

Lake's eyes were feverish. He seemed to be gathering himself. Culver backed to the desk and the man took one step forward. Culver stopped.

"Careful. This thing might go off!"

The smile had left his face and Lake suddenly seemed to get the idea that the automatic might go off. He wet his lips nervously, took a step backward and then sat heavily in the chair that Culver had indicated. Culver kicked a light chair out into the middle of the room so that it was between him and the agency man. He lifted the sheaf of paper slips, holding them so that he could look at them without relaxing his watch over Lake.

The very first one brought a snort of satisfaction. It answered a question for him. It was a report form of the Bridwell Agency, Timothy Carr, Operative, and it was a report on the movements of one Richard Richards. Culver's eyes hardened.

"So you buzzards lied to me? The bird who got the bump tonight was not one of your men; he was a competitor. And he was tailing your client while you were tailing his. Sweet."

Culver's voice dropped and he leaned forward. "Why did you knife him, Lake?"

The sweat glistened on Lake's white face, but his lips twisted defiantly. "Are you crazy? Why should I—"

"That's what I want to know." Culver stood up and crossed the room, towering over the man in the chair. "You killed him. He didn't tell me he was a Mack man when he asked me to sub for him. You believed that, didn't you? It could have happened. A private dick might use another agency's name to keep his own dark. Okay. But he didn't. When he mentioned the Mack Agency, he mentioned the name of Phil Lake, and he was dying when he did it. I thought that he was giving me his name. I knew different when your boss told me his name was Carr."

Lake was gripping the arms of the chair tightly, his lips pressed hard over his teeth. "I don't know anything about it."

"No? How did you and Mack know all about it when I came in. The cops hadn't found the body yet. And they wouldn't call up a competing agency to tell you, would they?"

"What do you want? Where's your angle?"

Culver smiled grimly. "Now we're getting somewhere. I want to know why Carr was rubbed. I want the lowdown on this Indian killing. There's someone bigger than you are in this mess. I want to know—"

"You working for Bridwell?" Lake's voice was strained, harsh. Culver shook his head.

"You thought so when you saw me in the park and saw Carr talk to me, didn't you? Thought maybe he was teamed." Lake's face told him that he was right. He nodded. "That explains the delay in coming up here. You didn't figure it safe until I walked in like a rube and explained myself."

**HE SHIFTED** the gun experimentally. "You've got ten seconds to talk and talk fluently, Lake. I want the whole story. I want to know where Carr tied into the Indian kill and who is behind the whole mess. If you don't chirp freely, I'm going to beat the truth out of you and throw what's left to the cops."

"It's none of your business. You aren't in it."

"Carr hired me to sub for him. I'm still subbing. Talk!"

There was yellow in Lake and it was showing now; it showed in his haunted eyes, in the sweat that bubbled on his death-like face. He fingered his lip nervously, his eyes on Culver. When Culver took a step toward him, he shrank back.

"Wait. I'll tell you, but—"

"No buts." Culver's jaw was hard, his eyes narrowed. He took another step forward.

The phone rang noisily.

For a moment Culver stood rigid. Lake started up and sank back. His lips were blue. "It's the cops," he said hoarsely. "Mack was going to call."

"You didn't talk soon enough. You...."

Culver stopped as the agency man's eyes widened. Lake was coming slowly to his feet, a mingling of relief and astonishment on his face. "Sure," he said. "I didn't talk. What if I did? Let the cops come. You're the boy in the spot, Mister. They know me. All the cops know me. And who are you? A Chicago hood with false references in our file. Maybe you killed Carr. Maybe I caught you here in his room. Maybe—"

Culver cursed softly. He had known what Lake had just discovered long ago. If he hadn't, he wouldn't have waited for the cops; he'd have phoned for them. Now the infernal phone was ringing and the cops were coming and Lake was wise to himself.

He lashed out suddenly with the gun and Lake caught it coming in. The agency man went down in a heap and Culver stepped back. With a deft motion, he dropped the gun into his pocket and swept the sheaf of reports off the desk. In a quick stride, he was across the room. His finger clicked the light button and the room went dark. He dived for the door.

There was a clanging sound out in the hall as an elevator door opened. He stepped back, his hand tightening on the gun.

It was too late now to make a break. The cops were already in the hall. He darted to the window, pulled back the shade and looked out. Mack was hurrying across the street. He was evidently worried that his call had not been answered. He'd be up in a minute and what a sweet job he and Lake could do on Culver. No cop in the world would give the man from Chicago a hearing with the story that he had to tell.

The knob clicked as somebody tried the door; then a key grated. Culver sucked in a deep breath and stepped through the window. There was a narrow ledge about eight inches wide running across the hotel front. The wall jutted out about six feet to the left of the window and formed a niche. Shaking inwardly, Culver eased along the ledge and balanced himself in the angle, his hands pressed hard against the wall on two sides of the V. Beneath him there was scarcely room to stand. His heels were planted firmly but his toes stuck out over space. There was a four-floor drop straight down. He didn't look. He knew it was there.

In the room he had just left, the light blazed on.

# CHAPTER FOUR
# DEVIL'S NEST

THERE WAS a sound of heavy footsteps in the room coincident with the turning on of the light. Pressed hard against the wall close to the open window, Culver could hear only a series of grunts and monosyllabic sounds, but he knew that there were two men in the room. He swore softly.

"Some day," he said, "some genius is going to make a sound strip of two coppers grunting to each other and prove that Darwin was right."

The hall door banged and Culver could hear the entry of Think-nothing-of-it Mack. The agency man simply burst upon the room. He let out a loud groan over the fate of his operative and then rasped off into a streak of plaintive rather than robust cursing. Another heavy voice, no long grunting, cut him off.

"Stow it. What was this ham sleuth of yours doing in this dump. Who slugged him?"

Lake was evidently coming to. Culver could hear him moaning and he smiled grimly as Mack stalled for time. The big boy wanted Lake to hear his story so that they would check on it. The man with the heavy voice was impatient.

"Kick in. You're holding us up, Mack. This is a murder rap."

"Murder? No!" Mack's voice was properly surprised; then Lake came out of it. His words tumbled out. He had come up after Culver, had found him searching the apartment. The guy had slugged him.

"Who in hell is Culver?"

"Chicago hood maybe. I didn't suspect. I've been imposed upon." In plaintive, sorrowful tones, Mack reeled out his story. Culver had come to him with references and a story of having an inside lead on the Indian's killers.

"I took him on, Brady. It listened good." Mack's voice shook with earnestness. "And I played it safe. I wired to Baltimore to check his references. Too late to phone. The wire is on file. You can check up. Lake and me trailed him here."

The man addressed as Brady snorted.

"That's the hell of you private dicks. A damned nuisance. Always messing up things. If you'd tell us when something funny comes up? But no! You have to—aw hell!"

There was a click from the phone and then he was growling into the receiver, talking to the desk. He turned back, evidently, into the room and closer to the window. His voice was more distinct.

"We're going to have a little fire," grated Culver. "They may find your body afterward."

"I'm going down and check over the late arrivals in this dump. Probably somebody planted here to watch Carr. Find anything, Dave?"

The other H.Q. man had been silent up till now, evidently on the prowl through the apartment. His voice was slow, heavy. "Not a thing. A guy lived here; that's all."

The phone rang and Brady barked into it. His voice rose a little. "The devil he did? Well, you lock both the doors out of this joint right now. Tell that eight ball to stand by. I want to talk to him."

The receiver clicked. "The desk," he grunted. "Shine janitor saw a guy come in from the alley. Didn't see him go out. Come on Dave, we'll give a look."

"My head hurts. I got to rest," Lake was moaning.

"Rest all you want to and see if I care!" Brady was stamping out. The door slammed. There was silence in the room.

For twenty ticks of a watch there wasn't a sound. Culver was becoming a little dizzy on his perch, a little cramped in the muscles. Mack's voice broke the silence.

"You played hell, Lake."

"Stow it. The guy came in like Dempsey and it was that mugg, Culver. He's no tramp. Someone planted him on us. Listen."

In terse sentences he outlined the charges that Culver had flung on him. Mack paced, his heavy foot tread plainly audible through the open window. At length he swung to a stop.

"I'm going down stairs," he muttered. "Those dicks might turn the egg up. We got to watch our step."

"Yeah. And we better step, too." Lake's voice held fear. "The quicker we clean up and scram, the better I'll like it."

"Washington isn't so good in summer." Mack sounded thoughtful. "Be back in a few minutes, Phil."

HE BANGED out and Culver eased his position on the ledge; bending his knees until he could feel his body weight pulling him forward and down; then he straightened. He clenched and opened his hands slowly and experimented with the leg muscles. Satisfied at last, he edged along the ledge and poised with one knee on the window sill. He heard a match scrape inside the room as Lake lighted a cigarette. He was through the window before the match went out.

Lake spun with a startled cry that died in his throat as Culver pulled down on him with the automatic. Culver smiled. "Talkative when I'm not around aren't you, Bright-eyes?"

"I— I—"

"Yeah. I know. Well, that's okay. You had your chance to talk to me and you muffed it. I'm not interested."

With a swift movement, Culver appropriated the box of matches in the man's hand. Very deliberately, and still keeping Lake under the gun, he whipped the desk blotter out from under the portable type-writer and wadded it into the waste basket with his foot. There was some more loose paper on the desk and he dropped that in on the blotter.

Lake was wide-eyed. Culver jerked a light blanket from the bed and crossed the room with it held loosely in his hand. He smiled at Lake as he struck a match and set the contents of the waste basket afire. The flame leaped up and he crammed the blanket in on top of it, leaving a channel for air.

"Make a swell bunch of smoke without hurting anybody," he said pleasantly. His mouth thinned. "But now you get on that phone and yell that there's a helluva fire up here. And act terror stricken, baby. Act terror stricken. I might leave you here."

Lake hesitated, took one look at Culver's face and jumped for the phone. The smoke was already swelling up blackly. He yelled into the receiver and his voice had the right note. Culver jabbed the gun into his back and liter-ally kicked him to the door.

"Out fast now!" He raced his man down the hall to the service stairway. Lake was perspiring heavily and there was caked blood on his face from the cut in his scalp. He did not look pretty and he was scared.

"But why…?"

"Stow it. You heard him tell 'em to lock up, didn't you? What am I, Houdini?"

Culver raced him to the third floor, paused a moment to smash the glass of the fire alarm there and herded him down to second. There was a lavatory there marked "Women" and Culver played on man's avoidance of such places. Even dicks on the search might pass up that door unless they had reason to do otherwise. Delicacy had nothing to do with it; it was merely a question of psychology.

Crouched inside the door, Culver heard the clang of elevator door, excited voices. Lake, with the gun in his back, was silent. The wail of a siren came from outside. There was an engine house a block away. Okay.

**PEOPLE WERE** moving in the hall now; tenants. Culver's lips tightened. This hideout was not as good as it had been. He could picture some scared female in a wrapper bounding in—a scream and blooie!

The mental picture disturbed him and he relaxed a moment. The gun did not press so hard and Lake was desperate. He twisted suddenly and dropped to the floor, his hands clutching for Culver's legs.

It happened fast. Culver spilled like a ton of brick and rolled over. Lake was on him, too busy for yelling; his long arms lashing out with desperate fists. Culver brought one knee up and threw him off as a bony left fist came down. The fist cracked against the tiled floor and Lake gave a sharp yip of agony. Culver heaved up under him, spun him half way to his feet and swung a right to his jaw.

With a sucking sound like a man going under water, Lake collapsed. Culver picked up the automatic that had dropped from his hand, stepped across the body and opened the door.

It was a tense moment but not as tense as if this were the fourth floor. Two detectives cannot be everywhere in the house and the chances were that they would be on four or in the lobby. Perhaps there was one in each.

A startled man in a bathrobe took a leaping side-step as Culver came out. He was temporarily the only one in sight. Culver stabbed at him with the gun.

"Out of that robe, you! Quick!"

"But—but— I can't— I—"

"Out of it!" The automatic moved. With a gurgling sound, the man shed the robe. He was stark naked. Culver grabbed the robe and gestured with the gun.

"Lam!"

The man was making little choking noises. He looked down at himself and turned like a scared rabbit. He lammed. Voices sounded around the L in the hall. Culver measured the distance to the red light marking the fire escape, decided against it and popped into an open doorway. There was no one in the room and he kicked the door ajar, crouching. A woman screamed down the hall beyond the L and there was the sound of running feet going the other way.

"Just a gal who can't take it. That guy was pretty bare."

Culver stuck his head out, breathed deeply and lined out for the fire escape. He had rolled his trousers up above his knees and his bare legs stuck out below the robe. He had it pulled tight under his chin. He threw away his hat and dived out the window.

The fire escape was a single weighted ladder for the last story. It swung down with Culver's weight and a patrolman materialized out of the alley gloom below, light reflecting off his badge.

"Whoa there. Nothing to be scared of. Go back. No fire."

The man was calling to him but Culver kept coming. The naked jaybird upstairs would be telling his story in a minute and Phil Lake would be hollering murder. The ladder hit bottom.

"You don't have to, I tell you. There ain't any big fire."

The patrolman was red faced, earnest. He was looking at the robe and the bare legs. Culver shook his head. "I got sent to hospital once, officer, because the fire wasn't bad enough to escape from. I'm going to look at it from out front."

He was puffing and putting on a shake act. The copper grinned. "You're going to feel bad coming back through the ladies," he said. "Yer ladder's gone back without you."

Culver looked up and favored the cop with a short grin. It had to be short. There was liable to be an unfriendly head sticking out of one of those windows any minute.

"Hang the ladies," he said feelingly. The darkness of the alley swallowed him.

He was snaking out of the robe even as he fell into running stride. The fire apparatus was puffing out in front and making a din, but through it he heard the high whine of a police whistle. He kicked his trousers down and came out of the alley with his hand caressing the butt of his automatic. There was a line of traffic held up by the fire wagons and half of the cars were empty hacks. He went into one like a homing pigeon. The hacker stared.

"Where to, Mister?" Culver grunted.

"Pick some place quiet where there aren't any fires," he said. "I want to think."

# CHAPTER FIVE
# TANGLED TRAILS

**T HE TAXI** rolled through tree-shaded streets in the residential district of Washington. Culver smoked a cigarette and stared thoughtfully at the back of the driver's neck. They turned into a well lighted boulevard and Culver grunted.

"Pull into the curb somewhere near a light. I want to read something."

It was the hacker's turn to grunt. "There's a dome light if you want it."

"Yeah. Well I've got a habit of reading under street lights. I'm not open to suggestions."

"Okay." The cab rolled to the curb. Culver took the sheaf of reports from his pocket and went slowly through them. Carr had been a painstaking shadow, but Culver read nothing that indicated a mastermind. If Carr was a menace to someone it didn't show in the reports. He was just another single track gumshoe who got on a trail and held it without trying to figure out what the motions meant. So anyway, the reports indicated.

He was on Richard Richards from morning till night. He reported minutely where the man ate and where he got his shoes shined and who he talked with; but there were no flashes of illumination. It was dry as dust.

Not till he was close to the end of the stack did Culver strike pay dirt. The report for the morning of the day on which the Indian was killed made him sit up straight.

Jimmy Troll, the Montana Indian who was supposedly a close friend of the murdered man, had visited Richard Richards, the lobbyist, alone.

Mike Wendell, the murdered Indian, had come in while the two were talking in Richards' office and there had been a row; the sound of angry words being plainly audible out in the corridor of the office building.

Phil Lake had come in during the row and taken a seat outside Richards' office. Mike Wendell, bouncing out alone, had discovered him there and there had been another row, more violent than the first.

Lake had been the last to leave Richards' office and he had left as the others had, growling and sore. Richards didn't leave for an hour afterwards and then he merely went to Harvey's for lunch.

Culver breathed deep and reached for a cigarette. He had an idea that Mike Wendell's death warrant had been sealed during that one stormy session. But who had sealed it?

He swore softly and wished that Carr had had flashes of intuition or sharp ears or something. The split between the Indians was a jolt and knocked a few of his theories in a heap. If everybody was mad, anything could have happened.

The police could even have been right. The Indian might have gone on a bender and been knocked off by some cheap guns just for the heavy dough he carried.

But there was Carr—

He was morally certain that Lake had killed Carr. But without a motive, the case felt flat. The Carr kill had to be tied into the Indian kill. It couldn't be lonely and make sense. If it was tied in, then that eliminated the stray stick-up man as a suspect. He tried to think through.

The Indian had Bridwell's agency tailing Richards to find out what Richards was doing about his visit to town. The Injun was no dummy. Okay. Richards had Mack's outfit tailing the Injun to find out who his connections might be. Okay again.

But why did Mack keep right on working after Richards called him off? And why did Richards call him off?

"It always comes back to Richards," he muttered. "The mess starts there or it finishes there." He rubbed his jaw experimentally. "That hood of his wasn't asking any questions before he moved my head out of the way, either."

His mind was suddenly made up. There was no sense in trying to think his way through the mess with the information that he had. It was no deduction job anyway; not for a man who was on the spot for the killing himself and who might feel a tap on his shoulder any minute. Not at all. In sheer self-defense, Culver had to wind this thing up; and brains were only incidental to the things he had to do.

He leaned forward and tapped the taxi driver on the shoulder. He had learned the name of Richards' hotel from the Carr reports. He gave the hacker the address and leaned back; his eyes narrowed, cigarette smoke curling lazily.

**IT WAS** a short run and the cab swung to the curb before the imposing hotel which had housed vice-presidents during their terms of office and visiting potentates and celebrities at all times. Culver wiped his handkerchief across his face and grimaced at the grimy deposit that it accumulated. He had a hunch that he didn't look like a visiting duke.

Well, duke or no duke, this was the stop-off. With swinging shoulders, Culver crossed the luxurious lobby.

There would be a staff of house dicks here and there would be a desk staff that knew something besides the winner of the fourth at Bowie. Nobody was going to crash a room by clowning a message and jotting down a number. The service stairs wouldn't be a prowler's boulevard either.

The desk clerk was sizing him up. Culver reached the desk. "Baggage coming through tomorrow," he said crisply. "Had a little accident coming in."

The clerk's eyes ranged from Culver's hatless head to the scuffed shoes, stopping en route for side trips along various creases in trousers and coat.

"I'm sorry," he said. "We are filled up. If you had wired—"

Culver's eyes were level, his voice cool. "I drove up here from Oklahoma and I picked this hotel because my friend, Dick Richards, recommended it. Is that your final answer?"

The clerk swallowed hard and stopped looking at creases. Oklahoma meant oil and oil meant money. Oil men didn't have to dress up. The Richards name was a clincher. He pushed the register across the desk.

"I'll try to accommodate you. Some reservations didn't arrive."

"Humph!" Culver gripped the pen and wrote in sweeping script "E. A. Howe, Tulsa." He flipped the register back with the mental note that the name could be translated "Easy and How." His lips, however, were tight.

"Fix me up on the same floor with Mr. Richards. Got a lot of business with him. See a lot of him while I'm here." He made his voice gruff, impatient. The clerk nodded and summoned a boy.

"You have 811, sir. Mr. Richards has 820 across the hall."

"Right." Culver turned to go; then, as if struck with an afterthought, he came back. "That chap Casson still with Richards or would you know?"

The clerk's eyebrows went up. "Mr. Casson occupies a room in Mr. Richards' suite," he said drily. He accented the "Mister." Culver smiled.

"Thanks," he said. "I knew that boy when he was a kid."

It was with an effort that he kept from whistling as he followed the boy to the elevator. Things were clicking and he was glad that he had not forgotten the name of Double Dick's bodyguard.

He owed Mister Casson a good poke in the jaw.

## CHAPTER SIX

## DOUBLE DICK SPEAKS

CULVER STOOD in the middle of the room and looked thoughtfully at the telephone. Time was a factor in his plans now but it was three fifteen ack emma; a bad time for getting things done. He could hardly walk across the hall, bang on a door and walk in. Flop house tactics were out in a spot like this.

He picked up the phone. "Room service, please." The phone clicked and there was a line hum. You didn't order through the board in a spot like this and "Room Service" took your word for your room number. A man's voice answered. Culver pitched his voice low.

"Three of White Rock and a bucket of ice to 820. Shake it up!"

"820? Yes, sir. Right away, sir." Culver smiled. He had an idea that early morning orders for set-ups were not so uncommon in the affairs of 820. Double Dick was a lobbyist, wasn't he?

Culver pulled a chair over close to the door of his room and sat there smoking. An employee of the hotel who thought that his mission was legitimate could make all the noise he wanted in the hall without bringing a house dick down on his neck. Culver would be conspicuous banging on the door himself.

He heard steps in the hall and the banging started. It was only about a minute and a half before the door across was opened. An angry voice, quite evidently that of the bodyguard Casson, cursed the boy from hell to breakfast. The door slammed. Culver stood up and opened his own door. A badly puzzled boy was starting back down the hall. Culver flagged him.

"Three White Rock? That's mine."

"Yours? The slip says 820."

Culver squinted, snapped his fingers. "Shucks. I bet I pulled that bone. Clerk told me my friend Richards' number same time he told me mine. I got 'em mixed. Too bad, son."

He was talking like an Oklahoman—or trying to—but it was the dollar tip that made the biggest impression on the boy. Culver ditched the bottles swiftly. There was an alert gleam in his eye. He had had to waste time on the kid but it was better than having a peculiar circumstance reported. That was fixed now.

He stepped across the hall, raised his knuckles and rapped sharply on the door of 820. There hadn't been time for Casson to go back to sleep and Culver heard him move. He rapped again and the sound of an oath boomed through the panels. A foot hit hard against the floor and the knob turned. Culver gathered himself.

The door was jerked open and, for a split second, Tub Casson's red face was a perfect target in the opening. Culver threw his right with his whole body behind it and the bodyguard went back four feet. Culver didn't wait for him to hit. He cleared the door sill and swung the door behind him. His left hand flicked the light switch and his right came out with the automatic.

Casson had pulled up short and dropped to one knee. He was staring stupidly, his eyes a trifle glassy.

"I owed you that, Wise Guy. Now be nice."

Culver shook the gun suggestively and walked down on his man. Casson shook his head groggily and got to his feet. He was wearing gaudily striped pajamas and there was no place for hardware. Culver didn't have to search him. He merely prodded him on through the nearest bedroom and into a room beyond.

The light in the other room flashed on and the tall, gray man who had got in the Oklahoma car earlier in the evening stood in the doorway. He had a gun in his hand and Culver covered him. The older man was carrying his gun loosely and he let his gun hand drop under the menace of the automatic. Culver nodded.

"That's nice. Now throw it on the bed and sit down on that chair over there, Mr. Richards. It'll be better."

**THE MAN** threw his gun on the bed, looked contemptuously at his bodyguard and defiantly at Culver. He sat down; his face stern, eyes steady.

"You know my name, so this is not accidental," he said slowly. "Who are you?"

"Just a guy with a gun and a lot of curiosity."

Culver waved the glowering Casson to another chair and sat down himself; the gun in his lap. Richards was white but undisturbed. "If you think that you are going to get away with these high-handed tactics—"

"The answer to that one is 'Yes.'" Culver was leaning forward; his own lips tight. "This call may be a friendly one. I don't know. You're in a spot."

The lobbyist challenged him with level eyes but did not speak. Culver held the spotlight. "An Indian who was in your way was murdered the other night right after you called off the agency that was shadowing him. That looked bad. I got slugged in the jaw tonight for merely trying to talk to you. That wasn't good. About the same time, a detective hired by the surviving Indian to shadow you was stabbed in the heart. That, Mr. Richards, was lousy!"

He was hunched forward in his chair, hurling the words. The lobbyist passed a hand across his forehead and the hand was shaking.

"You say that a detective was murdered, a detective shadowing me?"

"I said what you thought I said. A detective shadowing you was murdered. Now do you see why you are in a spot?"

"If you tell me just who you are and why you're here," he said slowly, "and if you'll put away your gun while you are telling me, I'll try to cooperate with you. Otherwise—"

"Never mind the otherwise. That's all I wanted to know." Culver pocketed the automatic. "Now, who killed Mike Wendell?"

"I don't know."

"All right. What was the row about in your office when Jimmy Troll called on you and Mike Wendell caught him at it?"

Richards started. He seemed surprised and instead of answering the question, he asked another. "Before I go into that, who are you? How did you know about that?"

"The name's Culver. Wendell had Bridwell's agency trailing you and a lad named Carr reported the fuss. Carr's dead. I'm following through."

"Oh." Richards lighted a cigar. Culver made a mental note that the man would be a great witness on the stand. "Troll was a Montana Indian interested in some Indian oil land developed by our company. Wendell was an Oklahoma Indian with much the same interests. The similarity stopped there. Troll was poor. Some of his Montana neighbors helped finance the trip. Wendell was very rich. He liked women, liked gambling and liked whiskey."

"Then what?"

"They both had an idea that they could get government pressure on my clients and obtain more money for their respective tribes. Troll was serious. Wendell was having fun. They split and Troll came to me. He offered to go home and stop seeing congressmen for a cash settlement."

"Did he get it?"

"He did not. Our leases are perfectly legal. Wendell came in and found him talking to me. He was quite angry and made threats."

"What kind of threats?"

RICHARDS WAS very grave now. He looked thoughtfully at his cigar. "He threatened to shoot both Troll and myself if Montana received better terms at the expense of Oklahoma. A very childish thing."

"Maybe. Well, Lake came in then. What about that?"

Richards shrugged, his jaw hard. "That fellow! He was hired by Mack to follow Wendell. He was stupid enough to come right into my office. Wendell recognized him and jumped at the conclusion that he was working for me. He went into another tantrum."

"How did he recognize him? Why?"

"Because," Richards bit the words off, "the fellow had been stupid enough to get into dice games and other games of chance with the Indian. It was imbecile handling of the affair and—"

"You broke off with the Mack Agency for that?"

Richards was startled again. "I did. Immediately."

"Swell," Culver was smiling now. "And I got poked in the jaw. Why?"

It was Tub Casson who answered.

"Because, Guy, no panhandler ever walked up a hotel driveway to stem a silk hat getting in a car. You got it for pretending you were a gimme when you weren't."

Culver looked embarrassed. Even the granite mask of Double Dick Richards relaxed. The phone rang shrilly.

"Which of you answers that thing usually?"

Casson looked at Richards. "I do," he said hesitantly.

"Okay. Answer it now. Don't get impulsive."

Culver was tense. The room vibrated as the man answered the phone. A pause and then he turned. "It's Mack. He wants to talk to you, Mr. Richards."

Culver relaxed suddenly. His mouth lost the hard lines. "If he wants to come up, let him."

Richards nodded. He crossed to the phone, talked in curt monosyllables. "All right, then," he said at length, "come on up." He turned to Culver. Culver's eyes were gleaming.

"Don't tell me. Let me guess. Mack's been trying to put the tap on you, hasn't he?"

"If you mean blackmail, yes. I wrote him a letter terminating his services in the Wendell affair. It was unfortunately dated just prior to the man's death. He photostatted it. He also photostatted the check that I gave him as a retaining fee the day that the Indian arrived in town."

"And you'd hate to have him turn those items over to a yellow newspaper?"

"I would. Indians, for some reason, are popular with the public. Oil companies are not."

Culver nodded. "Tell me something else. Why did you hire an agency to shadow one Indian—Wendell—and ignore the other one."

Richards shrugged. "I knew about Wendell in advance. The other one wasn't very important. I had an idea that he would follow Wendell's lead. He came in a day after Wendell did."

"Ah. I wondered about that." Culver was feeling suddenly like Sherlock Holmes. He had a deduction on the ice and ready to serve. He leaned forward. "If you'll call that other Indian, Troll, and make him come right over, and if you'll say what I tell you to say, I'll clean up this mess within the next hour."

The gray haired lobbyist raised his eyes. For a moment, he looked long and earnestly at Culver; then, seemingly satisfied, he nodded. "You do that and you'll have my check for five thousand dollars in your pocket when you leave," he said shortly.

## CHAPTER SEVEN
## THE INDIAN KILLER

CULVER WAS hidden in the other room when Mack came in followed by Phil Lake. The agency man was expansive, genial, hearty. He greeted the reserved lobbyist rather effusively and nodded at the silent Tub Casson.

"Can you send your man after cigarettes or something?"

"I can." Richards nodded at Casson who rose reluctantly. Lake, a little battered and the worse for wear, saw the bodyguard to the door and closed it after him. Mack lost some of his affability.

"Mr. Richards," he said, "that was a bad play tonight. Three people saw your man, Casson, strike Carr, a private dick, down in front of an apartment house on Sixteenth."

"Yes? You say the man's name was Carr; the man that Casson hit?"

"Right. The fellow was hurt bad. Casson used a knife on him. He got across the street near his car and collapsed. He's dead."

"That's absurd."

"We can prove it." Mack's voice was hard.

"Come to the point."

Mack's grin was forced. "I'm not a headquarters man. I don't have to make a case in court. I don't even have to play with the cops. I have certain information linking you with two murders. I'm turning that information over to the papers tomorrow unless—"

"Unless what?"

Mack's eyes were narrow. "The contract that you cancelled with your letter dated on a certain day, a day on which one of the killings occurred, is worth fifty thousand dollars to me. I accept the cancellation for a cash settlement."

"Very smart. The contract didn't exist and it wouldn't be worth that much if it did; but cancellation sounds better than blackmail."

"I stand by what I said. Your company will pay that gladly to preserve you. A lobbyist is never any good to anyone after he's been in a scandal. Not even if he beats the rap."

There was a click from the door leading out into the hall. Mack came to his feet. Lake pushed back his chair, his hand dipping for his shoulder holster. Casson came into the room with Jimmy Troll, the Montana Indian.

Looking through a crack in the door from the darkened inner room, Culver saw a short, squat man whose face was badly pocked and whose eyes were small.

"These gentlemen wanted to talk about the Wendell murder. I thought you'd be interested."

The Indian's eyes fell. "Sure."

Mack's usually placid face was lined viciously now. "Maybe you think that was a cross, Richards. Well, we'll see. You invited this guy. Now I'll talk in front of him. Maybe he wants something, too. And maybe you'll have to give it to him for being smart."

"Yes?" Richards was looking at the Indian and now he put a question that Culver had suggested on a guess. "You're a poor Indian, they tell me. Why did you keep on paying the Bridwell agency to shadow me after Wendell, who hired them, died."

The guess hit the bull's-eye. Jimmy Troll hesitated, then shrugged. "I wanted to."

**RICHARDS TURNED** to Mack. He had another of Culver's questions ready and Culver tensed against the answer. "Why did you force the issue on this question at this time of the morning? Why not wait till breakfast time at least?"

Mack's face was a little worried. He smelled something not on the program. "This latest killing complicated things and—"

"And I was running around loose." Culver stepped out of the dark room; his hand crammed deep into his pocket, fingers wrapped on the automatic. Mack kicked his chair back. Lake got his gun half out. The Indian blinked dazedly. Culver stuck his pocket out suggestively.

"As you were. You didn't crave having Richards and Bridwell get together, did you, Mack?"

"What do you mean?" The agency man was pop-eyed.

"I mean that Lake killed Carr, you mugg. Sit down, Lake! I mean that this whole thing was a plant, a graft. You smelled a shake-down opportunity when Richards hired you."

"This whole thing is a frame. Let's go, Lake. We'll go down to the *Herald.*"

Mack was trying to rise. His usually florid face was ashen. Sweat beaded on it. Culver waved him back savagely.

"You tried to shake down Richards when Wendell was killed. Troll tried it before Wendell was killed. Neither one worked. And you were pressed for time, Mack. Once Richards found out that the Bridwell Agency had been trailing him, had full reports on him from the moment Wendell hit town, well, you'd be sunk. No shakedown on a man that had a witness like Carr."

His eyes narrowed. "You wanted to eliminate that witness. His reports didn't mean much without his testimony. You wanted more than that. You wanted to kill him under circumstances that would tighten the noose around Richards. You didn't have to make a case for court. You just had to make a case that the public would believe, and that

Richards would know that the public would believe. Richards might have paid."

A look at Richards' face confirmed that. Lobbyists did not crave the spot-light. Mack was staring. Lake was ashen. He started to rise again and the action jarred Mack out of his lethargy.

"Let him rave, Phil," he snarled. "None o' this baloney is evidence."

Culver balanced on the balls of his feet. "Carr is killed and if Bridwell is made to believe that he was killed because Richards was guilty of the Wendell affair, that's swell for you. It keeps Bridwell and Richards from comparing notes and makes an enemy for Richards out of an honest agency."

Jimmy Troll was staring hard. He got up. "I know nothing about this. I go," he said huskily.

"Sit down!" Culver's voice had bite in it. "You lousy tramp, you never saw Montana." It was another guess and it hit again. "Mack hired you when Richards told him about Wendell coming. Just another angle on a shakedown. You may be redskin but you're phony other ways. Wendell was a playboy Injun. He was a cinch to fool."

The room was electric now. "Wendell carried ten grand. You, Troll, knew that. Lake got in a crap game to make sure for himself. That much was worth putting in the kitty. Ten grand plus fifty grand to Mack from Richards, plus something else to Troll from Richards."

**CULVER'S EYES** flickered to Richards. "Do you get it? You were the fall guy the minute you hired a shyster dick like Mack."

Mack was drooling at the lips. "None o' this is evidence," he repeated plaintively. "We'll make 'em say it in court. The cops will be glad to know this Chicago hood is here. Let's go."

He was starting up again. Culver's lips curled back over his teeth. "Here's evidence if you want it," he said grimly, his eyes on Lake. "Wendell had a big diamond. His murderer has—"

He never finished. Lake was lightning fast on the draw. The light flashed on his gun almost simultaneously with the dull boom. Culver fired through his pocket and he felt a bullet whip his cheek as Lake went up on his toes and spun.

In almost the same split second, he was aware of something else. A trifle slower than Lake but no less serious, Troll had gone into a hip pocket. The gun was coming up when Lake fired and when Culver fired. Culver twisted desperately and he felt death reach for him.

Automatics should not be fired from the pocket. The slide had jammed in the cloth.

Tub Casson launched himself like a football tackler. His thick shoulder hit the Indian as the man's finger tightened on the trigger. A mirror went to pieces as the slug hit it. Jimmy Troll hit the floor.

Culver was across the room in a stride. He took no chances. Literally tearing the gun out of his pocket, he raised it and brought the barrel down on the Indian's head. Troll went limp and Casson rolled over, a wide grin on his broad face.

"Thanks, Kid." Culver wheeled toward Mack.

The agency man had made no attempt to draw a gun. He was staring at Lake who lay face downward in a slowly widening pool. He was biting the end off a cigar and his face was very white. Richards, too, was white but there were iron hard lines around his mouth.

Culver stood irresolute for a moment; then he dropped on one knee and lifted Lake's head. The man had been drilled through the forehead. Culver shrugged away his repugnance and dipped into the man's vest pockets. He brought out a ring with an incredibly big stone and stared at it. Mack, too, was staring.

The agency man was still numb with shock. "The damn fool," he muttered. "The damn fool!" His eyes were on the ring.

"Evidence!" Culver said. "But? They both shot." He spun and crossed to Troll. The Indian was still out cold. Culver searched him. His face cleared and he turned to Richards. He held in his hand another ring; a duplicate of the first.

"That clears that. One of them is phony. One of the boys—I don't know which one—tried to cross the other. The play fixed them both."

Richards picked up the phone and called the police. Mack shook himself and put on his hat. "I'm sorry that one of my boys was crooked," he said piously. "I'll run along."

"You'll stay here and talk to the cops." Culver was almost cheerful. Richards turned from the phone, reached in a desk and pulled out a check book.

"Five thousand and cheap at the price," he said crisply. "What are those initials, Culver?"

"Just Dean Culver." Culver waved Mack back as he was starting once more for the door. The agency man cursed.

"I tell you, Culver, you haven't got a thing on me."

"We'll let you tell the cops."

"But, hell!" The agency man was buckling at the knees. "You know how cops are. They hate a private dick's guts. They—"

Culver accepted his check, lighted a cigarette and grinned cheerfully. "Think nothing of it," he said.

# THE MOBSTER MAN

THE BLUE BARREL ERUPTED HOT LEAD AND INFORMATION— WHICH WAS THE MOST DEADLY WAS A QUESTION UNANSWERED UNTIL DEAN CULVER WROTE THE SOLUTION IN FIERY LETTERS ON THE HEART OF THOSE WHO WORE THE DOUBLE CROSS AS A BADGE OF HONOR.

**THE NEWS** sheets of the old town were dull as only newspapers can be dull in the days and the weeks when crime news lags. The underworld like a gorged python lay coiled upon itself waiting. There were elections coming up and there was a big graft investigation under way. The politicians were busy and gang guns cooled while mobsters laid low.

Dean Culver thumbed the sheets over indifferently. He had been back in town more than a month, back after a year of exile. He stopped turning pages when he came to the first page of the *Press-Courier's* second edition. The banner spot on that page was the two column feature under a cryptic head *The Blue Barrel.* Culver smiled grimly.

That heading was his idea and the column was his idea and only he knew it. The *Press-Courier* itself did not know where the phoned items came from; the *Press-Courier* knew only that the whispering voice on the phone was the hottest tipster on the underworld that the town had ever known. What Winchell had done for Broadway, the *Blue Barrel* was doing for the underworld of another city. The *Press-Courier* took its increased circulation gratefully, featured the column and forbore curiosity.

But the *Press-Courier* had fired Dean Culver over a year before. It had fired him and turned him out disgraced after an underworld frame. A Cordo gangster had died under the guns and there had been "evidence" in his effects that branded Culver as a crooked reporter. He had been through then, and he had got out. Now he was back. His lips thinned.

The man who had framed him was the town's big political poobah, "Black Bart" Brunderson. Culver had played too hard. Well he was playing harder now and the *Blue Barrel* was his weapon. As the blue barrel of an automatic might stand for death, the blue barrel of the *Press-Courier* stood for exposure. And Dean Culver was shooting the deadly paragraphs. He was not a stool and the "square crooks" did not tempt his aim. It was too bad for the chiselers, though, and he was biding his time until the day when he could get Black Bart in the sights.

For several minutes he read, then he yawned and turned in. He had the faculty of dropping off to sleep immediately. He did not know exactly when he awakened. Something had stirred in the room. He lay motionless in the pulsating darkness. Cautiously, his hand crept along the coverlet until he felt the cold butt of his automatic under the pillow. Something moved in the shadows near the window.

"That's enough, you mugg! I've got the drop."

**CULVER'S VOICE** slashed through the brooding darkness that had settled after that one slithering sound. He heard a faint gasp from the shadows and his hand darted to the light socket beside his bed. Light flooded the room and Culver, eyes squinted against the sudden glare, saw a shabby little man who pressed back against the window with arms out-stretched. The intruder's face was pasty white and covered with unkempt gray stubble. Faded, washed out eyes pleaded silently. The man's mouth worked.

"I didn't—"

"Shut up! I'll do the talking."

Culver slid cautiously out of bed. His eyes ranged the room and lingered for a moment on the partly open window. He frowned. It was a good ten yards along a narrow cornice from the fire escape to that window. He looked again at that shabby stranger. It seemed inconceivable that such a poor specimen could have made the cat walk.

"All right," he said, "I'll listen to what you've got to say."

The intruder wet his lips. "I'm Beau Bridwell," he said. There was pride in the statement and the mere act of mentioning the name seemed to steady the man. He brushed his lips again. "You're Dean Culver, aren't you? I didn't make a mistake!"

Culver nodded. "I'm Culver and you made a helluva mistake."

"No. No." Bridwell looked around like a trapped animal. "I had to see you. Doc Bromley told me when I was going out that you were square. I had to see you and—"

"Yeah?" Culver was interested but he had no intention of letting the other know it. Doc Bromley had been a pretty decent crook and Culver had given him a good press when he got in trouble. "You had to see me, so you jimmied in. Swell. They've got doors on this joint."

"Sure." Bridwell's lips twisted. "It would look good for you, too, if I walked in and paid a visit." He laughed harshly. "When half the town is goin' to be hot on my trail tomorrow—"

"What for?"

Bridwell's face seemed whiter than ever. He wet his lips again. "I just left Judge O'Ryan's house. He sent me over for a double saw buck when he was trial judge and I swore

I'd kill him if I ever got out. The papers published it when I said it." He took a deep breath. "Well, the Judge is dead."

Culver's eyes widened. *"You killed O'Ryan!"*

"No. No. I swear I didn't." Bridwell was trembling again. "I was in the house but I never touched him—"

"Sit down. I want details—and fast." Culver moved to the window, looked out along the narrow ledge and then crossed to the door. Satisfied that no one else was showing any exceptional interest in his affairs he came back and sat down. Bridwell was fumbling with a cigarette.

"The governor gave me a pardon last Tuesday," he said dazedly. "A full pardon. The papers raised hell. Seems like

the same day he signed the pardon, there was a meeting of the parole board and they voted nix on giving me a parole."

"I read about that. Go on."

"Well, I was just as balled up as the sheets and I've been wondering ever since. I didn't have no mouthpiece working for a pardon, no politics in back o' me and no dough. Howcome, then, I get pardoned when the governor's running for re-election and giving me a pardon means him getting hell from the papers?"

"I'll bite. Why? But get along to this O'Ryan killing."

"Come on in," growled that hard voice as the gun prodded Culver's back. "We'll have a real party now."

**BEAU BRIDWELL** shivered slightly. "I don't believe in nothing that I don't understand," he said slowly. "That there pardon o' mine was screwy somehow and I got worried. I figured maybe O'Ryan was back of it and had maybe some new facts or something—"

"Yeah? Did you do the job that you went up for?"

Bridwell shifted uneasily. Dean Culver waved. "Okay. You were guilty as hell. Go on."

"Well, there ain't nobody better at opening up a box than I am, even if I'm out of practice." Beau Bridwell's thin shoulders squared. "And I figured maybe there'd be a tipoff in O'Ryan's safe on why I got that pardon. It had me screwy worrying about it being some kind of frame and I had to know."

Culver nodded, his eyes narrowed. He could understand that. Bridwell took a deep breath. "I jimmied in as easy as buyin' a drink but I wasn't no more than in the place when I hears a noise and it's between me and my getaway. I fade out into a dark hall and then I hear somebody moving upstairs, too. There ain't no place for me to go, so I back into a little mop closet under the stairs and just wait. Then I hear somebody comin' down the stairs and he goes right into the study where I'd just left; the place where the safe is. There's a lot o' quick action in there and he gets the light on; then I hear him give a quick choking kind of sound and he falls. I can hear his body hit."

Beau Bridwell wiped his forehead. "That was just hell for me. I figure that it's the judge that's come down the stairs and here I am in his place when he gets socked; me, the guy that swore to kill him."

"Yeah. That's exciting. How did you know he was killed?"

"I looked in afterwards. They was awful still for a while and then when nobody else showed up, they started to move around again. There was two fellers in there and maybe three. I crawled to the door and the judge was sprawled out on the floor. There was a lantern on the floor in front of the safe and a feller working for the combination. Me, I crawled up the stairs and found a window that went out on a porch. Then I came here—"

Dean Culver was jumping into his clothes. "You mugg! Taking all that time to come to the point and those crumbs still working on that safe. Hells bells!"

Bridwell's jaw dripped. "What are you going to do?"

"Do? I'm going out there. Here, throw these on. Fit you too much but that's all right."

Culver tossed a well worn suit across to the bewildered Bridwell. He flipped a pair of twenty dollar bills after it. "When you get those rags on, drift right out the front way like you owned the place. Do a quick blow to Mother Mason's. You know it, don't you?"

The little crook's nod was enough. Most old timers knew Mother Mason's. Culver was slipping on the harness that held his armpit holster close to his body.

"Okay. Mother Mason's. And keep your mouth shut. Give her *both those twenties* and tell her I sent you. Then wait! You interest me and maybe I'll go all the way with you."

A quick flip set his gray felt in place and he snapped the brim; then he was gone. Beau Bridwell wet his lips.

## CHAPTER TWO
## THE MURDER ROOM

**THE HOME** of Judge Michael J. O'Ryan was a gloomy pile of gray stone that stood in an acre of ground just inside the City line. Culver slipped through the row of trees that paralleled the auto driveway and circled to the back of the house; every sense alert to signs of alarm either inside or outside the house. The judge, he knew, was a widower who kept only two aged servants in the old house and a chauffeur who slept over the garage. There was little chance of the murder being discovered until morning as long as it had not already been discovered. Still, it was not a sure bet. He circled the house warily before he moved on the window in back through which Bridwell had entered.

He had no intention of stepping into a trap at the scene of a murder, but he had a powerful urge to visit the scene before the police tracked up the place. He hardly dared to hope that the safe had proved tough and that the intruders would be still there—if they had ever been there—but he granted that it would be more than interesting to come across the men at work.

For Culver knew—as all the city knew—that Judge O'Ryan had spent nearly six months digging up evidence of graft and corruption on the state government in its dealings with the municipality. Quite conceivably, there were a number of persons who would breathe easier if the Judge breathed no more.

Not a sound disturbed the suburban quiet of two A.M. as Culver tested the window. It moved easily under his hand and it was only the work of seconds to raise it and step over the sill. Then, in the black darkness of the old house, he stood and listened. Somewhere a clock was ticking noisily and he could hear the insignificant sound of water dripping somewhere from an imperfectly closed tap. Other than that, he was alone with the beating of his own heart. He glided forward, his eyes accustomed now to the darkness, and found himself in a big room that was probably the dining room. At the far end there was a door leading off a hall. He stepped through and crouched low when he saw the stairway. His eyes narrowed.

There was a little mop room under the stairs just as Bridwell had said, but it was much easier to get out by way of the window which he had used as an entrance than it was to go upstairs.

At the foot of the stairs and to the left, there was an open door and Culver moved toward it cautiously. His hand closed over the butt of his gun and he balanced lightly on his feet, then he looked in. Darkness shrouded the room but he didn't need light to tell him the obvious thing. There was no one in there.

Some of the tension went out of Culver then and he stepped into the room. His hand found the flash on his right hip and he turned it toward the floor. A little circle of light stabbed the darkness; darkness that suddenly became a tangible, living thing; black shuddering gloom that pressed upon the challenging beam of light and struggled to engulf it, to hide from it the thing that lay on the floor.

Sprawled there on the floor just two steps in from the hall lay the body of a man, his arms spread wide, fingers clutching emptiness.

**CULVER'S LIPS** tightened in a straight line and he dropped to one knee. The man's face was almost buried in the thick nap of the rug and Culver moved him gently. The pencil-thin beam of light moved over rigid features, strong even in death, across the sparse gray hair and then stopped. High up on the man's head was a horrible wound; horrible because the skull had not withstood the blow.

"The Judge all right. Bashed his skull in. Never knew what hit him. Length of gas pipe maybe." He was puzzled at the manner of the murder. The job did not look modern. It didn't have the professional touch.

"I wonder now. I wonder." He moved across the room and located the wall safe. His flash played over it and he recognized it as a good one. It showed no evidence of having been worked on. Not a scratch violated its shiny surface. He tried it with a gloved hand. The door was locked. He circled the floor about the safe with the probing flash but found nothing significant. Once more he let the flash wink out and sat down in a big chair.

His nerves were tense, but he felt that he was on the verge of drawing cards in a very big game and that he was justified in staying on the premises until he had checked all the angles. There was a chance of police interference, but the chance was so slim that he discounted it. They wouldn't show until someone called them. If they did— well, that would be too bad.

"Either that mugg, Bridwell, was so scared he got mixed up or he deliberately lied. Why?"

Culver let his eyes wander in the direction of the hall door. He couldn't figure any reason for Bridwell going up-stairs to get out of the house. "Any jury would hang him," he said slowly, "and I don't know but what I would, too. There could have been three other fellows here—but were there?"

He got up and crossed the room toward the body and then stopped with a jerk; every faculty suspended, a strange crawling sensation running along the surface of his skin.

The tomb-like stillness of this room of death was being shattered by the shrill, clamorous ringing of the telephone.

For the space of a heart beat, Dean Culver stood rooted; then he took a quick step toward the desk and lifted the receiver. There was no conscious reasoning in the decision; sheer instinct warned him that the ringing of that bell would bring the household and that he would be trapped— or given at best a short start on the baying hounds of the law. For all he knew, of course, the damage was already done, but he had to risk that.

"Judge O'Ryan's residence." His voice was well under control.

"Long Distance. Capitol City calling Judge O'Ryan."

"Sorry. His honor cannot be disturbed."

"Wait a minute." The girl's voice seemed to fade out, then he heard her in a sort of faraway conversation. "Sorry, sir. They say that Judge O'Ryan cannot be disturbed." Then a heavy, masculine voice cut in.

"This is Governor Barker. It is imperative that I speak to Judge O'Ryan at once."

CULVER'S EYES glistened with a strange intensity. He heard the girl ask the governor if he would speak to whoever was on the line and the sharp affirmative; then the voice was demanding.

"What is this about not disturbing the judge for a long distance call?"

"He left orders, sir." Culver was sparring for time. He felt as though he were chained to that murder room by the slender thread of wire. To hang up would be to direct instant suspicion or—the phone would start jangling again.

"Orders be hanged. This is Franklin Barker speaking, Governor Barker. Do you understand?"

"Yes, sir."

"Say, who is this?" There was suspicion in the governor's voice. Culver took a deep breath. He might, he decided, gain a few precious minutes by a bold stroke.

"This," he said slowly, "is somebody who has no business in Judge O'Ryan's residence. I came here and found something that I had nothing to do with. Judge O'Ryan is lying dead in his study. He's been murdered."

He heard the governor's quick intake of breath and his swift ejaculation of shocked dismay. He waited for no more. The long distance operator was probably plugged in. Whether she was or not, it would not take long for the governor to raise the alarm. He whipped the receiver onto the hook and darted for the exit.

"I'd give something pretty to know what the governor wanted with O'Ryan at two-thirty in the A.M." he whispered. "There's a real angle to play on."

He was over the window ledge with one quick writhing motion and the tree shadows swallowed him as he made his way rapidly to the car that he had parked two blocks from the grim stone house. As the powerful motor whirred him toward town, he could hear the police sirens wailing. He smiled cynically.

A murder was about to be officially discovered.

Two minutes later he was in the phone booth of an all night drug store and a frantic staff at the *Press-Courier* was tearing up the Home Final that would be at every door in the morning. The two column strip from section two was being slapped around and the *Blue Barrel* was on the front page with another beat.

# CHAPTER THREE
# AT ZORRO'S

**T**HE DAWN was still an hour and a half away when Culver stepped down a short flight of steps to the basement entrance of a once magnificent residence. A door swung open and the sounds of music drifted along the dimly lighted passageway that led to the rear of the house.

To the public, this place was Diamond Dan's; a place where one might dine and dance and drink better than average liquor at any hour of the night, a deluxe spot that had never felt the heavy hand of the raiders nor the fetid breath of scandal—in short, a well-nigh perfect speakeasy. To the underworld, this was "Big John Zorro's," a place on the "Word of a Sicilian." It was a place run out of bounds as far as the police were concerned and no man, no matter how badly wanted, was subject to the fear of arrest while he was on the premises; by the same token, gangsters might take their ease in the same room with sworn enemies and not fear lead. It was a confidential place and things might be arranged there. It was, in short, the pulse beat of the underworld and the man who knew how to read signifi- cance in little things might forecast the future from a ring- side table at Big John's.

Culver was interested in the underworld's pulse rate tonight. The murder of Judge O'Ryan was going to rock the crime world to its foundations and the smart members would be drifting in for veiled discussion. He did not, however, get his ringside table.

Big John himself bore down upon him as he stepped into the big room. "Ah, Culver, my frien'. I am glad to see you in-a my place. Always I am-a glad to see you—"

"Yeah. That's the old come-on baloney for the suckers, John. What's on your mind?"

Big John seemed pained. He shrugged a fat pair of shoulders. Careful barbering had not taken the greasiness out of his skin and there was a dirty stream of perspiration rolling down his fleshy cheek. He passed his fingers lightly across his full mustache and the gesture seemed to wipe away the grimness that had lingered momentarily in his face. He grinned widely.

"Always you joke, Culver. That is fine. Me, I laugh and kid with everybod'. Sure Mike. Fine feller with all the boys— Smile all the time, that's a-me, Zorro."

"I'll sign a paper and swear that's right; but spit out the works, John. What's the lay."

Zorro's manner became confidential. He leaned forward. "Some good friends of yours, Culver, they want they should see you in room 'C.' Right away they want they should see you."

Dean Culver's eyes narrowed. "Spill the names, John."

Zorro shrugged. "The boss," he said. "The Mister Brunderson."

Culver digested that. He nodded his head. "Much obliged. I'll go right up, John."

The Sicilian grinned and bobbed his head. He seemed relieved as he hastened away to spread the glad hand to some new arrivals. Culver lighted a cigarette and inhaled slowly.

"The old sinner knew that there wasn't any friendship in that call from 'C'," he said. "He kind of hated to give me the message. Oh, well. We'll look."

**HE STROLLED** slowly to the stairs. At the head of the short flight, he turned into the long dim passageway and paused outside of the door marked "C." He took out a fresh cigarette, stuck it in his mouth and held a cigar lighter in his hand as he rapped on the door.

It opened wide and he smiled grimly as he looked into the eyes of the man who opened it; Vito Torino, boss of the city's second largest mob. The only other person in the room was black Bart Brunderson, the political power behind many thrones. Culver dropped his lighter into his pocket, took out a match, and lighted his cigarette. He nodded indifferently to Torino and fixed his eyes on Black Bart.

"Heard you were looking for me. Right?"

Heavy jawed, slightly bald and larded with a good forty pounds of excess weight, Black Bart was a formidable figure. He was rolling an unlighted cigar along his lips and his eyes were drawn in behind narrow slits in the big pouches that surrounded them. Torino, a beautifully barbered youth, closed the door softly. Brunderson grunted.

"We been talking about you, Culver. We ain't sure we like you."

"No? That's a damn shame, Brunderson."

"No foolin', it's a shame." Brunderson's cigar stood straight out from suddenly tightened lips. "O'Ryan got the bump tonight, Culver, and that raises hell. This here is a census. You were washed up on the news sheets a year ago. What's your racket?"

Culver's eyes were narrowed. "Do I have to have one?"

Brunderson glared. The cigar did a quick, rolling round trip along his wet lips. "The waltz don't get you anything," he said. "You play around the hot spots and you're working for something or somebody. You don't print your dough. You'll either lay your cards on the table with me, Guy, or you'll find you're in the wrong town. Get it?"

Culver let the smoke curl lazily from his nostrils. His eyes held Brunderson's. "What will happen?"

It was like a slap in the face. Black Bart straightened. His fist hit the table. "Happen? You lame-brained punk! Everybody knows you ain't regular. Everybody knows that the papers are off you. What does it leave? Bah! You know what happens to stool-pigeons."

Culver laughed. "Come again. You know I'm not a stool and you didn't get where you are by taking wild swings in the dark. What else have you got that I'd be interested in?"

Vito Torino cut in before the apoplectic Boss could answer. His voice was soft. "You mus' not play the damn fool, Culver. Always when a man will not do business, there is the bump—"

The air of easy badinage that he had worn in dealing with Black Bart dropped from Culver as he whirled toward the gang leader. His eyes bored into the little wop who played the cards of double-cross and murder for high stakes.

"That's just fine, Vito," he said crisply. "There's a phone down the hall. You call up Pete Cordo and tell him that you are going to put Dean Culver on the spot. Go ahead. Call him!"

**THE GANGSTER** wet his lips and looked toward Brunderson. He made no move toward the phone. Culver laughed and turned to the door. "Glad to've seen you boys," he said. The door slammed.

Outside in the discreetly dim hall, however, Culver was not smiling. He took two steps, doubled back and leaned against the door of the room that he had just quitted. He heard Brunderson's booming voice.

"Why didn't you call Pete Cordo?"

Then the shrill, womanish voice of the excited Vito. "Not me, Boss. This Culver, he must not be bumped. Cordo says that. Some day if you and me—"

The voice dropped, faded out. Culver glided away, hesitated at the head of the stairs and then walked down confidently. The big room was filling up. There was the usual quota of hilarious parties and a more than normal number of quiet, hard-eyed men who sat at tables without women. Culver took a table in the corner and ordered dinner. His mouth was hard.

It was a tough spot. No matter how lightly he may have taken it in Brunderson's presence, it was not funny now. Culver had been biding his time against a clash with Brunderson. He wanted power in his hands next time and he was not ready yet. Brunderson still held the power that a politician always holds; the power of the frame. And Brunderson had an ally now with another kind of power; the power of the Tommy gun.

Between Culver and the first danger, there was nothing but his own wits. Between Culver and the guns of Vito Torino's mob, there stood only Pete Cordo. And Pete Cordo had reason to hate Culver as much as he feared him.

Culver had an idea that his mention of Cordo had been a mistake. He shook his head grimly and looked up.

Black Bart Brunderson was swinging across the big room alone; headed for the door. Culver's eyes narrowed.

He had a sudden hunch to follow along and acted on it. Brunderson was going through the wide doors in front when Culver stood up.

## CHAPTER FOUR

## TWENTY-FOUR

## HOURS TO LIVE

**C**ULVER CAME briskly up the steps from Zorro's and hesitated at street level. He had lost Brunderson. A long dark sedan moved from the curb half-way up the block and moved toward the spot where Culver stood.

It moved like the shadow of death itself and he had no time to get under cover. His hand darted to his armpit and he crouched back against the building front. A voice snarled from the shadows:

"None o' that. Walk out nice."

He was covered. He turned his head slightly toward the voice, then swept his eyes front. He couldn't see the man who had spoken and the car was in front of him now. He drew a deep breath and stepped out. A man stepped out from the shadows behind him and stuck a gun in his spine. He moved toward the car. Pete Cordo glared out at him. Beside the big shot of gangdom sat Bart Brunderson. Culver let his breath out slowly. This wasn't a bump then; this was an inquisition. He bowed mockingly. Brunderson was grinning.

"I been telling Pete how you're goin' around braggin' that there ain't nobody big enough to bump you off."

Culver looked at him coolly. The lights in front of Big John's were bright enough to allow him to read faces. "Have I been bragging?"

"You told me that Pete Cordo wouldn't let you get bumped, didn't you? That's bragging." There was a vicious intensity in Black Bart's voice. Culver turned to Pete Cordo.

"I told that cheap little perfumed cannon o' Brunderson's—Vito Torino—that he couldn't do it," he said slowly. "Am I right or wrong, Pete?"

Cordo had a broad, Slavic, unintelligent face. He frowned and shifted uneasily. "Nobody talks for Pete Cordo. I don't let nobody say what I will do." He didn't look at Culver. Brunderson cut in fast.

"You're probably holding something Pete wants, Culver," he said. "But that won't get you anything with me and Pete working together. You're going to spit clean about who you're working for or you're taking a long ride. Pete's not backing you worth a damn."

Culver shrugged. He did have something on Cordo and he had not hesitated to use it in a world where men fought with any weapon at hand. He would have scorned to take blackmail money, but he had needed the security that had been his by virtue of Pete Cordo's fear. Now that security was being threatened and his life wasn't good for an hour under present circumstances with the hand of Pete Cordo against him.

He had seconds to come to a decision about Brunderson and his interest in the affair. Brunderson lived for politics and he lived for power. He was not taking a lot of time tonight, of all nights, on the affairs of Dean Culver unless he, too, was afraid; afraid that Culver's racket was political. Black Bart's activity tonight was a give-away. He had something at stake, something with which he feared interference.

In a flash, Culver's decision was made. If he was important to Brunderson, it was because Brunderson had a weakness in his armor someplace. Brunderson was afraid, despite his bluster, and a man who has something big at stake and who fears to lose it is a prime customer for a good bluff. Culver's teeth flashed in a smile.

"I'm not walking away from here into any bump, Brunderson," he said softly, "for the same reason that I haven't been bumped before. Pete played the sucker by letting you get in on him, but Pete is still protecting me for the good of his own hide. Get that?"

**BRUNDERSON ROLLED** the cigar and turned to Pete Cordo. Cordo's face was sullen. He was between two fires and he was beginning to realize that he hadn't played the game like a big shot. It made him angry and red spots glowed in his cheeks. For the first time he met Culver's eyes. His brutal lips curled back from his teeth.

"Culver, you maybe haven't got what you say you've got. I got to see it. If you got it, you let me see it. If you don't let me see it—then by God, you have not got that thing!"

The words came hard as though pumped out by a brain unaccustomed to framing long sentences. Culver's lips thinned. "Cordo," he said bluntly, "you know what I think of you. You're a dumb mutt and not too terribly tough. But you're big, Cordo, because you keep your eye on the ball and you don't make the mistake of getting brainy. That ain't your game. You run your mob in words of one syllable and thoughts of one syllable. When you get in with a bird like Brunderson, you're hearing words you never heard before and you're getting your brain into things it don't understand. Lay off!"

Black Bart's eyes widened and the cigar slipped from his lips. "What the hell—"

His voice trailed off. Pete Cordo had lifted his head and his eyes were flaming. Culver had played his cards well out of his knowledge of those who live by guns rather than gab. Pete Cordo could understand the double cross when he couldn't understand anything else. His mind, as elemental as an animal's, was easily reached by a suggestion of treachery. He was suspicious by nature; dull witted and painfully conscious of his mental inferiority. As Culver had pointed out, the very secret of his power lay in his dull mind. The agile brains of politicians had not been able to ensnare him because he had refused to engage in any duel of wits. Tonight he had departed from his custom because Brunderson had pretended to know more than he did know about Culver's hold on him; a bluff that the politician was already regretting. Cordo hadn't missed that crack about Torino either.

Brunderson was breathing hard, but fighting for the poise that is the armor of the Boss. He wasn't big for nothing. "Pete," he said, "this guy is one smart cookie. His one play was to get between us and he pulled it off. I pay off on him, but—"

Cordo waved him down. "Pete Cordo talks for Pete Cordo," he growled. He was no longer undecided. There was a heavy frown on his broad face. He leaned toward Culver and his eyes glittered.

"Culver," he said, "I have never see what you got. I mus' see it. If you got this thing, we talk business. If not—" he spat. "I give you twenty-four hours—"

Culver lighted a cigarette. He could run a bluff still and Cordo would be uncomfortable, but it would do little good.

Pete Cordo had a single-track mind. Culver looked up at the fading stars.

"Okay, Pete," he said quietly, "I'll bring you photographic copies."

**HE TURNED** on his heel and walked away. He walked confidently but there was a chill wind along his spine. "I've got twenty-four hours to mess this thing out someway," he murmured. "Twenty-four hours—"

It was a very short time for Dean Culver had bluffed and he had not a thing in the world to show Pete Cordo.

He had reached the corner now and he looked back. Cordo's car was breezing away and Black Bart Brunderson was standing on the pavement looking after it. Culver smiled grimly. If he had done nothing else, he had accomplished one thing. With a whisper of suspicion, he had erected a wall between Cordo and Brunderson. His enemies, at least, would not be together. He turned and walked toward his apartment.

Once upon a time, there had been in existence a paper with the signature of Pete Cordo; a paper that would change the map of the underworld if it were published. Pete had signed it when he was a rising young thug and before he had even dreamed of being a big shot. He had signed it in Culver's presence after Dick Dayne, a private dick, had beaten the whey out of him. And in that paper he had ratted on six of his pals. Two of them burned in the chair because of information that Dayne got from that paper, but the confession had never been used as evidence.

Dayne had been killed in an accident but the paper never showed up. Cordo had jumped to the conclusion that Culver had it and he had credited the reporter with enough sense to plant the paper where it would go to the news sheets at his death. And he had been afraid of Culver after he had first got that idea; afraid of him as he was afraid of no one on earth.

Pete Cordo was big but not big enough to stand against evidence that he had once ratted on his pals, that he had committed the unpardonable sin of welching to a bull. He was calling a show-down now because Brunderson had caused him to doubt. He was probably wondering why Culver had never asked money from him....

Culver shook his shoulders as though to shake away the thought of what lay ahead of him. He had no illusions of what would happen to him in twenty-four hours. Pete Cordo would remember all of the years through which he had carried a fear of Culver in his heart and he would not be merciful. He had been known to amuse himself for days with victims who had incurred his personal hate.

Culver turned in at his hotel and made his way to his room. He sighed wearily and dropped on the bed. "Brunderson, Torino and Cordo already," he muttered sleepily, "and the cops maybe, if I stick with Bridwell. Swell opposition. Swell—"

With a grunt, he went off to sleep. He had nerves like that.

# CHAPTER FIVE
## THREE THIRTY—
## MOTHER MASON'S

THE JUDGE O'RYAN murder was a press carnival. There were columns of dope, most of it manufactured out of whole cloth; heavily leaded editorials, pages of pictures. The loud cry was raised for Beau Bridwell, but the opposition press had subordinated the subject of the ex-convict and turned the fiercest blasts upon Governor Barker. Why had he defied the parole board and released a man sworn to kill Judge O'Ryan? Did the Judge's investigation of the governor's appointments and the promised revelations in the wake of the investigation have anything to do with that strange pardon? The opposition press wanted to know.

The administration papers were defending the governor valiantly with very little to go on. They pointed out that Judge O'Ryan was the governor's life-long friend and that there was no evidence to support the idea that the Judge's investigation would involve the governor in anything discreditable. They did not try to explain the Bridwell pardon but they skirted it by pointing to the fact that it was a personal phone call of the governor's which had resulted in discovery of the murder.

All of the papers were up in the air about the identity of the man who answered the phone in Judge O'Ryan's residence. Culver grinned, flipped the papers aside, and went to call on Beau Bridwell.

Bridwell was pathetically glad to see him. His hideout was a narrow room partitioned off in the basement of Mother Mason's. It was a grimy, dingy, damp and uncomfortable hole but it was practically police-proof and some distinguished fugitives had found it a haven. The little crook literally pawed him for news. Culver looked at him.

"They're after you hot," he said bluntly. "But tell me something. Are you tied up with any of the mobs?"

Bridwell's eyes widened. "No. I steered away from everybody till I came to you. I was away nine years, you know, and—"

"You didn't recognize any of those bozos at O'Ryan's?"

"Nope. Didn't even see 'em clear. It was dark and they had their backs turned when they got near the lantern."

Culver's eyes were suspicious. "The safe didn't look like it had been touched."

"No?" Bridwell seemed genuinely startled. "They were in front of it when I lammed out. Unless—" He frowned.

"Unless what?"

"Somebody might have been able to open it by the feel. You know— Listen to the tumblers." He shook his head sadly. "There never were many that could do it, and I guess maybe there's less now."

"Could you open a safe like that?"

Fear shadowed Bridwell's eyes for a moment. He gulped a little, nodded. "Yes. Even big boxes and trick construction stuff like the Judge's." Pride banished the fear as he spoke and he seemed like another person altogether. Culver shot a question abruptly.

"Bridwell, did you kill O'Ryan?"

The little crook jumped, threw a terrified glance at the door. "No. No. I swear I didn't."

"Well, you're holding back something. Come clean!"

"No. No. I swear. I told you the whole story, Culver—"

**THERE WAS** deadly fear in Bridwell's face, the fear of a man whose fate lies in the hands of another. Culver could destroy him with a word and he knew no reason why Culver should protect him if it came to a jam.

Culver's eyes were still probing the washed out little man's face. Something eluded him. The man was honest in his answers and yet there was something still to be explained, some angle that Bridwell touched or controlled and of which he refused to speak. Culver did not believe that Bridwell had killed the judge not that he knew the murderers, but he knew something. Yet with his very life at stake now, if he wouldn't divulge his knowledge to the only ally he had, there was some factor in the case that Culver would have to unearth for himself.

He was on the verge of challenging point-blank on the point of Bridwell's escape from an upstairs window when the way to the downstairs window was open. He checked the impulse, however, as a sudden flash of inspiration came to him. There was a question that he had forgotten to put to Bridwell; a perfectly straight question and one that hit straight at the heart of the O'Ryan murder. It was so obvious that he had glossed right over it and yet the O'Ryan killing could not be explained nor solved until that question was answered. And Bridwell, he felt, held the key.

There was an exultant gleam in Dean Culver's eyes, and if the threat of living only twenty four hours had not been hanging over him, he would have forced an answer to his question from Beau Bridwell on the moment and saved himself an uncomfortable train ride. As it was, he merely laughed tolerantly.

"Stick it out, Kid," he said. "I'll be dropping in later."

He was still smiling when he left Mother Mason's but the smile froze on his lips as he started down the steps toward his own car. Directly across the street there was a long racy touring car with the side curtains up. Such cars had a sinister significance now. Culver's eyes narrowed. He could feel fingers of ice moving along his spine, but he knew that there was no advantage in retreat. He moved steadily down the steps.

Cordo's twenty four hours weren't up but there was always the chance that Vito Torino would get brave and bull the show; especially now when his patron, Bart

It was a snatch in the best gangland fashion. Pete Cordo's men had struck again.

Brunderson, had failed in an attempt to deal with Pete Cordo.

Culver's feet touched the pavement and nothing happened. He stood for a few seconds looking at his own car and calmly lighted a cigarette. Still nothing happened and he turned casually and walked across the street to the dark car.

**THERE WAS** only one man in it; a man as old as Bridwell whose face was coarse and puffy and whose eyes were, for the moment, fish-like, although Culver had seen them different. There was a silly, uncertain smile on the man's face, and he gripped the wheel tight. The engine was turning over. Culver nodded.

"How are you, Dick. Waiting for someone?"

The man looked doubtful, at a loss for words; as though things were not happening as he expected. "Yeah," he said. Culver grinned. He knew Dick Harper of old and it was one of the minor mysteries of the big town how the brain-scrambled old-timer held his place in a young and coming mob like Vito Torino's. A booze fighter who had once been something in the world of crime, Dick Harper had been down to the extremity of rolling drunks in the gutters and begging dimes along the big stem when prohibition came in. Now he had money and a job in a good mob and no more intelligence than a baby monkey with which to justify what he got. He wasn't even tough. His fellow mobsters took most of his money away from him when he got a split and nothing was ever done about it.

Culver was no wiser than anybody else and Harper had never interested him enough to prompt investigation. Today, however, he was glad that Dick Harper was a member of the Torino mob and that fate had delivered him into his hands. He smiled disarmingly.

"You wouldn't kid me, Dick," he said. "You were waiting out here because Vito saw me go into Mother Mason's and got curious. He figured that if he left this big bump wagon out here, I'd be plenty scared and hop right into my wagon and streak. Your job was to follow me and find out where I went. Right?"

Harper was staring dazedly and Culver chuckled. "You're a pretty swell hack herder they tell me."

Dick Harper's drink-dulled features lighted for a minute. "I'm the best that Vito's got," he said.

Culver knew differently, but he let it ride. When he got a sucker patting himself on the back, he kept him patting till his arm got tired. He was already shaping Dick Harper into his plans.

"Dick," he said soberly, "that's just the point. You're not only the best hack herder in the outfit; the only man they could trust to follow me on a getaway, but you're an old timer. You played the game when Vito wore diapers. You ought to be the brains of the gang."

Dick Harper's dead eyes came momentarily to life. He glowed for a second and then went as cold as a discarded cigar butt. "They don't trust me," he said bitterly. "Figure I'm too old."

"That's where they're foolish, Dick. Keeping you on small stuff."

Harper stiffened. "I don't just do small stuff," he said defensively. "You were talkin' about bein' the brains. I do big stuff. I—"

**HIS THIN** jaws snapped shut. Dean Culver's eyes narrowed, but he didn't press the point. "I'm going to give you a break, Dick," he said, "to show you I'm on the level with you. I'll tell you where I'm going. I'm going to go down to the station and buy a ticket to Castleton. I've got a girl out there and I'm going to lay low. Cordo is a bit off me and I want to give him chance to cool off."

He was watching the old-timer narrowly and he saw that the Cordo information was not news. Harper knew about it, and it scored by convincing him of Culver's truthfulness. There was a suspicious look in the bloated face, however, and Culver played to that look.

"You can follow me along and check up, Dick," he said. "I expect you to. You're smart and I know you don't believe anybody till you're shown. That's right."

Harper glowed again and his guard was down. Culver leaned closer. "Now I'll give you a real tip. Be back here about three thirty tomorrow A.M. and watch the door of Mother Mason's. You'll see something, Dick, that will make Vito and all the rest of those young squirts take their hats off to you when you tell them."

Dick Harper wet his lips and Culver saw that he was hooked. "Is that the goods?" he whispered huskily. Culver laughed.

"I am not getting paid for lying to you, am I? I don't stand to win anything, do I?"

He stepped back before Harper had time to ask any further questions and he heard the man mutter. "I'll be here, Culver. Thanks."

He laughed and walked across to his own car. There was nothing in Dean Culver's code of ethics that made it a crime to kid a bum like Dick Harper. There was no slinking, murderous gangster job that Harper wouldn't lend himself to, and, despite that muttered "Thanks," he'd sink a knife in Culver's back tomorrow for a bottle of cheap hooch.

With the dark car following him, Culver drove straight to the station, parked his car, and bought a ticket to Capital City. He was not worried about the possibility of Harper checking his ticket buy. A sloppy yegg of the Harper stamp would take his destination as Castleton for granted as long as he fulfilled the easily checked-up part of his statement and drove directly to the station.

"There's some good reason for having Harper in that mob," Culver said thoughtfully as he entered the train shed, "but it's one helluva mistake to use him for anything but the reason that makes him valuable, whatever the reason is. Vito Torino tries to get his money's worth and this is one time when he gets more than he bargained for."

His brain was already busy at the weaving of a web that would catch a choice bunch of flies when the clock in Mother Mason's banged three-thirty.

## CHAPTER SIX
## THE LITTLE BLACK BOOK

THE PRESS had been unable to reach the governor for an interview. He was not at the executive mansion, and his secretaries professed ignorance. Dean Culver didn't let that worry him. He had a little black book in which he had made jottings over a long period of years on the papers. There was quite a little about Governor Barker.

Under the heading of "Friends" there appeared the name of Dennis Slattery. To Culver, the item was a tip-off. Slattery owned the Parkway-Plaza in Capital City. It was a swell spot for a governor to lie low incognito. Under the heading of "Peculiarities" there was another significant item on the Governor. "Smokes Russian cigarettes in preference to cigars."

A small item! And it had been a dreary job assembling such trivia about hundreds of men in the public eye. Occasionally though, as now, the book paid big dividends. The first thing that Culver did at the end of the three-hour train ride to the Capital was to buy a package of Russian cigarettes at an exclusive cigar store. The second thing that he did was to empty the cigarettes into a refuse can. He kept the package and went to the Parkway Plaza, where he registered under his own name.

He was back down in the lobby five minutes after being shown to his room. He eased up to the cigar stand like a nervous man who is timid about making known his wants.

"I don't suppose you have what I want," he said hesitantly. "I generally carry a supply but they are hard to get...." His voice trailed off and he fumbled the empty cigarette case out of his pocket.

The cigar clerk frowned as he tried to follow the vague and hesitant preamble; then he squinted at the package and smiled.

"Ah, Russians! Well, you're in luck, my friend. We don't usually carry them. No call for them generally; but a gentleman up in 702 wanted them and I laid in a few. Glad now I did."

Culver was conventionally pleased as he bought his package of Russians. Inside he was laughing silently. He had succeeded easier than he had hoped. The best that he had anticipated was that the unusual request presented in an apologetic manner would lead the man to make some comment that would give Culver a clue to follow up; maybe by way of the Bell Captain. A governor in retreat, of course, would not buy cigarettes himself; he would send down for them. Culver turned away.

"Room 702," he said softly. "Well, now for a plan of the hotel and I'm set."

A distant, unseen clock was chiming eleven when he walked down the quiet hall of the seventh floor and stepped out on the fire escape nearest to the governor's suite.

The lighted battle monument two squares away looked unreal. The street below was a residence street and it was quiet, indifferently lighted and exceedingly remote. Down the sheer face of the hotel, there was shadow; sliced in two or three places by the yellow gleam from the lighted rooms within. Culver looked at the narrow coping that he must walk to the Governor's suite and shivered. He was no acrobat, and he would have preferred dangers with which he was more familiar, but there was no alternative. He shook his shoulders impatiently and stepped out.

**SEVEN STORIES** of empty space yawned under him. The blare of a taxi almost rocked him from his perch. His toes and fingers cramped and the sweat beaded on his forehead; then the darkened window that was his goal loomed ahead of him. He rested his palms on the sill and tried to forget the yawning space behind him. With appreciation, he noted that the window was part way open for ventilation. Balancing carefully, he widened the aperture, slid his foot over the sill and stepped into the velvet darkness of 702.

As was to be expected, 702 was a suite. Culver found himself in the parlor, and he was grateful for the breathing space. Carefully he wiped his hands in a handkerchief and worked the stiffness out of his fingers. He felt the automatic in his shoulder holster and eased the tiny flashlight from his hip. Moving softly, he crossed the floor to the connecting door which was open, and stepped into the bed room. Heavy breathing guided him to the bed.

He stood there for a second, and then pressed the button of his flashlight and sent a stabbing beam of light into the face of the man on the bed.

The lean, well moulded features of Governor Franklin Barker were revealed in the spot of light, and Culver gave an inward grunt of satisfaction. There was always the outside chance that he had made a mistake. As the beam of light hit him, the governor shuddered and blinked his eyes open. Startled, he half raised himself in the bed.

"What's— what's the matter?" he gasped. "Who...."

"Take it easy, governor. No loud chatter. Nothing's going to happen to you." Culver's voice was hard, commanding. The governor, fully awake now, stared into the light as though trying to see beyond it. He was remarkably self-possessed for a man awakened so abruptly.

"Suppose we have a little more light so we can both see," he said. His hand came up slowly to the reading light above his bed, but his movements were deliberate and he waited for permission. Culver nodded.

"Okay, if you watch your step. Might as well be comfortable."

The reading light came on and Culver pocketed his flash. The eyes of the two men met. Culver had his automatic in his hand. He moved it slightly and his voice was almost apologetic.

"If you tell me that I don't need this thing for self protection and give me your word on it," he said, "I'll put it away."

The governor smiled. "I'm curious, and that's your guarantee," he said. "I'll give you my word, if that's all you want, that I won't take any measures except in self-defense."

"Okay." Culver pocketed the automatic and stretched his legs. "This is the only way I could get an interview with you. I'm the guy that talked to you over the phone the other night."

The governor stiffened and his face paled perceptibly. Culver read the thought that passed through his mind and gestured impatiently. "Judge O'Ryan was dead when I got there," he said. "That's why I want to talk to you. I didn't have anything to do with it and I don't think that Bridwell did."

Franklin Barker relaxed. "You're not Bridwell, then. Mind if I smoke?"

He looked around him and Culver dipped into his pocket. "No, I'm not Bridwell, but I know where he is. I've got some of your favorite brand here. Take 'em."

**THE GOVERNOR** looked more bewildered than ever as he accepted the proffered package of Russians. "This is an extraordinary experience," he said slowly. "If neither one of us is crazy, it makes it even more extraordinary."

Culver was measuring the man through narrowed eyelids and he liked what he saw. Franklin Barker had courage and intelligence. He had undoubtedly been a tool of the political machine, but, if he had, it was because there was no other way of gaining the heights in the career he had chosen. No man became governor unless he pleased the politicians, but Culver was beginning to understand the pressure which had led to the O'Ryan investigation. Barker, once he was in power, would be a hard man for the ring to control. They had to trick him.

"If anyone is crazy," he said, "I'm it. Before I ask you for anything, governor, I'm going to trust you with a long spiel that's got personal and confidential written all over it."

The governor was looking at him curiously. "Thank you," he said.

Weighing his words carefully, Culver plunged into the account of his activities on the night that O'Ryan was killed. He related Bridwell's story, the appearance of the room and the subsequent events at Big John Zorro's. The governor listened gravely and Culver applauded him silently for the way in which he masked his emotions. Here was a poker player.

"There's the deal to date," he concluded, "and you can play with the police if you want to. I can't stop you once I leave here. But the police in the big town take orders from a lot of people who might not be your friends. I'm willing to be on your side because I can do myself more good that way."

The governor smiled. "Frank enough. What do you want?"

Culver's face was grim. "This thing means your official life," he said bluntly. "It means the only life I've got. I can do you an awful lot of good, and you can do more than a little for me if you come clean. Why did you give Bridwell a rain check?"

" 'Rain check?' Oh, you mean that pardon." The governor frowned thoughtfully. "You can't quote me because you never saw me officially. I can prove that nobody has talked to me." He lighted a cigarette. "I pardoned Bridwell because Lee Hodgson told me that the parole board was voting the recommendation. He called me up and said that he was anxious to expedite matters because Bridwell's mother was dying and that, out of sympathy, some fellow crooks of his had placed evidence in Bart Brunderson's hands that proved Bridwell to be innocent of the crime he was expiating."

Culver stared incredulously. "You fell for that?"

The governor shook his head. "I appointed Hodgson, but I wasn't that careless in an election year. I called Bart Brunderson."

**CULVER STRAIGHTENED.** His eyes were gleaming as he leaned forward. "So Brunderson isn't trying to elect you? That bothered me. Go on. They both denied later that they had ever mentioned Bridwell to you, of course."

The governor nodded. "Certainly. That's the first time that I knew that Brunderson wasn't behind me. O'Ryan warned me, but I guess the best of us make mistakes...."

Culver was frowning now. "You're the state ticket of Brunderson's party," he said. "What's he throwing the party for in a national election year? He backed you at the convention that re-nominated you."

The governor's eyes were half closed. "He did back me at the convention. That threw me off the track. Does it mean anything to you that our party has control of the Big Town with no election for a year there, and that our party is practically certain to elect the national ticket this year? That if I went over for another term, our party would control every bit of political nourishment in the state practically; national, state and municipal?"

Dean Culver sat silent with his eyes on the governor's face. Suddenly he clenched his fist. His eyes lighted with unholy joy. "I get it!" he said. "I've been blind as a bat. The other party's been in control of Federal money for years, and the bosses have traded favors with Bart Brunderson. He doesn't want them washed out of this state because there might be a new gang if they ever got back in power, and he'd be in the cold."

The governor grinned appreciatively. "That's it exactly." His face hardened. "He's willing to throw the state and ruin me to let the opposition put their candidate over and keep a place open at the public trough. He'll have enough graft with Federal patronage to dispense, and with his stranglehold on the big town." His jaw hardened. "He hasn't had any too rich pickings up state anyway."

Culver relaxed in his chair. The whole story was unreeling in his brain like a moving picture on a screen. It was not Franklin Barker who was menaced by the O'Ryan investigation, although the investigation had been forced as a frame for the governor. O'Ryan had warned Barker. That meant that he had stumbled across something that gave him a clue to what Brunderson was trying to do. He had tried to warn the governor, but he probably hadn't had enough to back up his advice—or he was waiting for more data to develop.

"Why did you call O'Ryan in the middle of the night?" Culver's voice was sharp. The governor's eyes clouded.

"I was working on a speech when I came to the conclusion that we've reached tonight. It came to me suddenly that the Judge's life was in danger if it occurred to anybody that he might be a menace to the little grab that was being planned."

**CULVER NODDED.** "A lot of men have been blotted for less than the 'take' that Brunderson's gang gets every year. Well, governor, I'm much obliged, and you won't be sorry you talked."

He rose to his feet and the governor eyed him speculatively. "You don't think Brunderson killed him?"

"No. I don't. There's no reason why he should do any dirty work."

"Well," the governor's eyes clouded, "I don't see what particular good this talk did you. What I've been telling you is not evidence, you know. No court would admit the statements I have made, nor the conclusions you've drawn. Why, even the newspapers would laugh. As for the public? Well, you know what the man in the street would say about my story of this affair."

Culver nodded. "I know. It's because there is so much mileage between fact and evidence that things have to be done the way I do them. The public wouldn't understand me, either."

"But what do you propose to do? What can you do?"

Culver's face was grim. "I'll ask a question first. The District Attorney down in the big town is an awful pain in the neck to Brunderson and his crowd. I think he's a damned pussy-footer myself, but he's got guts enough to buck the machine. Can you do anything with him?"

The governor frowned thoughtfully. "I might if I could convince him that Brunderson crossed me and that I'm not trying to frame him. I'd have to know what you wanted, though. I don't want to make a deal with him unless I have to...."

"Well, if you can do it and you're gambler enough, tell him I'm going to be in touch with him and that I'm shooting square—for him to do just what I tell him to do even if it looks like political suicide."

"I am afraid that will be hard to do."

"I know it," Culver walked toward the door and stopped. "You're a gone duck in this state unless you can do it," he said crisply, "and it's only a matter of time till that D.A. is framed nicely, too. Think that over."

"And if I can do it?"

"Well, in that case—and provided that I can keep Pete Cordo from rubbing me out—I'll smash Bart Brunderson so wide open that he'll never bother you again."

The governor sighed. "I wish I could believe you," he said. "But, believing or not, it's worth the gamble. I'll see what I can do with Mr. Joyce."

# CHAPTER SEVEN
# DEATH RIDE

IT LACKED a couple of minutes of three A.M. when Culver left the upstate train at the Big Town terminal. There was a telephone booth in a corner of the big station and he made for it. The number that he spoke into the mouthpiece was a number used by a very few people; the private number of Pete Cordo. For a few seconds he waited, and then a sleepy voice growled into the transmitter and Culver grinned. In a voice deliberately thickened he growled back.

"Cordo? Well, never mind who this is. I got dope for you. How'd you like to have the papers that O'Ryan was killed for?"

He felt the tension at the other end of the line. Pete Cordo was taking a few seconds for the question to sink in; then he swore.

"What you do? Kid me? Who's 'is?"

"Cut the fool questions. I'm telling you enough. Beau Bridwell is hiding out in Mother Mason's downstairs room. You know about that room, don't you? He has the papers ditched some place and Culver is making a deal to sell 'em to Brunderson. Torino's mob is going to protect Culver from you if the deal goes through. Get that?"

Culver grinned again as he heard Pete Cordo curse in thick gutturals. Nothing could be better calculated to wake him up than that crack about Torino protecting anybody that he wanted to get. Cordo was growling into the receiver again.

"How do I know this is not a kid? Who is 'is?"

"I'd be crazy to tell you who this is, but you can check up on the rest. There's one of Torino's men watching Mother Mason's in case Bridwell decides to blow. Better pick him up. You'll tip your hand if you burn him down. Those papers are worth a million to you, Cordo."

"But why you give me something like that? What the hell? This is one big kid. Who is 'is?"

"Aw to hell with you, you dumb ape. Stay in bed if you don't want it."

Culver clicked the receiver. He was grinning broadly now. There wasn't a chance in the world of Pete Cordo staying in bed. He might be doubtful but he'd check up. Once he found that the salient features of the story clicked, he'd be in for everything he had.

"I didn't kid him much at that."

Culver sobered as he faced the gamble that he would have to take himself. He was in control so far but any one of a number of little things could turn the tables on him fast now—and he was playing this hand with blue chips. His life was on the table and he had cards to draw.

He retrieved his car which was parked near the station, and drove to within a block of Mother Mason's. Hugging the shadows, he traversed the rest of the way on foot. The neighborhood was badly lighted and that helped. He entered the alley on the corner below his objective and came up the alley until he was behind the rooming house; then he slipped between two houses and traversed an area-way to where he had a good view of the street.

**THERE WAS** a man loitering in the shadows across the way and Culver gave a grunt of satisfaction. Dick Harper was on the job. He'd been a little leery of Harper but the man had taken the bait hard. The stage was set for Cordo.

The first intimation of the great one's coming was a second shadow that slipped out of a dark slit between the shabby old houses across the street. Dick Harper, unsuspecting and slow-witted, was not aware of that shadow for several seconds after Culver first discerned it. Then it was too late. Something rose and fell swiftly and Harper slumped. The other man caught him just as a big car swept around the corner.

With a faint rustle of tires against the curb, the big car came to a stop. For seconds nothing happened. Cordo was cautious of traps. One of his body-guards, a squat gorilla-like shape in the dim streets, slid out of the tonneau and looked carefully up and down the street. There was a low whistle from across the way, and the look-out turned. Culver recognized him as Hymie Katz, a lightning fast man with the gun and notorious as the killer of Bump Edwards; the killing that had made Pete Cordo the czar of the underworld.

Walking with a rolling swagger, Katz was crossing the street. In a few seconds he came back with the man who had laid Dick Harper low. They were carrying the slumped form of the Torino gangster and without any wasted motion, they dumped it in the back of the car. Nothing alarming had happened and Pete Cordo got out, a hulking giant who towered above his henchmen. Culver sank deeper into the shadows as the three opened the rusty gate and started quietly along the flagged walk toward the back of Mother Mason's. He had them all tagged now; Cordo,

Katz and Monty Morello. There was only one more factor to reckon with; the driver of the car. That undoubtedly would be Bill Gregory who was the ghost of a dream gone wrong. Gregory had once bossed Kerry Patch and had had ambitions; now he was Cordo's star driver and glad to be alive.

Culver's car was not far away and he had a chance of following this crowd if he had to, but it would be a risky play. This was no collection of ham talent. They would spot a trailer in a very few minutes and that might be sorrowful. Culver also had a gun and a good chance of sticking up Bill Gregory. He was about Gregory's build and he might get away with taking the fellow's place. He was very doubtful, though, about getting accurate dope from Gregory on where he was to drive; even with a gun as persuader. He'd be in a very bad spot if he drove to the wrong place.

A slight scraping noise sounded along the stone flags that ran around Mother Mason's. A second or two later, three men emerged into the semi-gloom of the badly lighted street. Cordo walked alone but the other two dragged another man between them; a struggling mite of humanity who had been roughly gagged and partially trussed up—Beau Bridwell.

The driver was leaning out of the car. Cordo, with a quick glance up and down the street, snapped his fingers. The driver's head disappeared and the two men swung their burden swiftly into the back of the car. Cordo stepped over the squirming body and Hymie Katz swung in beside him. Monty Morello was getting in beside the driver. Katz reached out to slam the door and Gregory ran the engine up.

**AT THAT** moment, Culver came out of hiding like a leopard on the leap for game. He had shed his shoes and he moved close to the ground with a terrific burst of speed. The door slammed and the engine roared. Culver leaped for the split-type rear bumper, locked his arm in the spare tire, and hung on. The car leaped away and he could feel the wrench in his shoulder sockets until he established his balance and swayed with the motion of the big eight. He was hanging almost straight out as they whisked around a corner, then he bumped back and the car leveled out....

Twisted pretzel-like on his insecure perch, Culver was not visible from inside the car. There was always a chance that a policeman or a late prowling nitwit of a pedestrian would call attention to him, but he discounted that risk as negligible. The hour was late and Cordo was not likely to drive along the brightly lighted boulevards with two prisoners on the floor at his feet.

Swinging off the smooth macadam, without warning the car jounced for three blocks over a mad causeway of cobblestones. Culver gritted his teeth. "It's better than the kind of a ride that Cordo would like to take me on." The sentence bounced in his brain; then the car roared off on a fairly straight street that had paving of a sort, slithered around a corner and straightened out. Culver forgot his discomfort. The route could only lead to one spot on the Cordo map.

"The cider mill!" he muttered. His eyes lighted with satisfaction.

Several miles beyond the city limits, and located in a deep depression between two embryo hills, the cider mill had once been an integral part of the crude system adopted for the making of liquor in the early days of prohibition. Secrecy had been necessary in those days and no one could approach the old mill in a car without advertising himself well in advance, nor could a sufficient number of men constitute a raiding party or stage a surprise attack. Since the liquor business had come out in the open, there had been little need for the cider mill, but the underworld knew that a couple of the Cordo "rides" had ended up there and that Pete Cordo still used the ramshackle group of buildings for purposes of his own.

They were rolling now over a country road; narrow and rutted. Culver could not look ahead of the car but he tensed for the moment when they reached the turn-off. The car jolted and there was a growl as the driver shifted gears. Culver let go, rolled over, and pulled his body flat at the side of the road. He saw the tail light of the car lift and then bob away as the big car turned off and started down the rough tortuous road that led to the Cider Mill. He spat a mouthful of gravel and smiled grimly. He'd gotten away with the big risk and he had nearly a mile to walk and then—

He left future events to the future and started down the road in the wake of the car; a scarcely perceptible humming sound now in the distance.

# CHAPTER EIGHT
# AT THE CIDER MILL

A SCATTERED pile of crumbling stone ruins beside a dry stream bed; that was the Cider Mill. A group of mound-like hills surrounded it. To the right of the mill proper was a blackened area of charred ground where a house had once stood, behind it and to the left the trees grew thickly. Laced through the trees and hung in double layers from deeply imbedded posts in front of the old stone pile was the barbed wire.

Dean Culver crawled through the wire above the blackened area and noted with satisfaction that there was a light showing on the main floor of the old dive. No curtain, shutter or shade dimmed that light and that simplified his problem. After all, why should Cordo be careful out here at four in the morning?

A few minutes of cautious movement brought Culver within range of that window. Nothing else seemed to move in all creation. The car loomed black and deserted some twenty-five yards away. A hum of voices came from the direction of the window. Pressed against the damp wall, Culver edged toward the lighted square. He could hear the voices now; rather, he could hear Pete Cordo's heavy guttural voice.

"Come through, yuh mutt! We know you got them papers o' O'Ryan's."

Bridwell's thin, frightened voice carried well. "No. No. It was all a frame, I tell you. I don't know anything."

There was a tense silence; then Cordo's voice again. "Got them things hot?"

Culver's lips were tight against his teeth. His fate was riding on a few words now; his whole scheme, perhaps his life. He risked a look through the window.

Hymie Katz, with a vicious look of anticipation on his face was turning from the fireplace with an ice tong in his hands. The tips of the tongs glowed red. Across the room sat Pete Cordo, a cigarette hanging on his loose lower lip, his eyes squinted malevolently in the direction of Beau Bridwell. The shabby little convict lay on the stone flooring, his hands and feet securely tied, a look of wild terror in his faded eyes. Hymie Katz started across the floor toward him. Pete Cordo waved his hand.

"Stick one o' them prongs in each of his ears. If he won't talk, he won't listen neither...."

Culver's nerves were taut. He eased the gun in his shoulder holster and wet his lips. Bridwell was wiggling frantically as though he would crawl away from the fate that was bearing down upon him. Suddenly he screamed.

"Keep it away. Keep it away. I'll tell you. I'll tell you!"

Pete Cordo's hand went up. He leaned forward and spat toward the terrified man on the floor. "Chirp quick!"

Bridwell was strangling with terror. "I took the papers," he moaned. "I got them. I cleaned the box before those other guys got there. But I didn't croak the judge. I swear I didn't croak the judge. I...."

"The hell with the judge. Where's the papers?" Cordo was breathing heavily. Bridwell looked at him wide-eyed. Culver was quivering. This was what he wanted. He'd suspected that Bridwell had those papers the last time he talked to him. He'd let him run to get two birds with a single shot.

"The papers are out at O'Ryan's, in a little tool house. There was a lot of them. I ditched 'em after the other guys croaked the judge. I could take you to 'em. They're safe there...."

**CORDO WAS** squinting at Bridwell with a look of cold malevolence. "That better be straight," he growled, "or getting hot pincers in your ears will just be play to what you'll get...."

Culver relaxed and hugged the wall beside the window. Cordo was growling again. "What did you want the papers for, you mugg?"

"I don't know. I don't know." Bridwell was obviously blown up. "I figured that pardon I got was screwy. I thought

"Sorry for the intrusion," droned Culver. "But move a
muscle, Senator, and you are a dead man."

I'd have something to make a deal with if they tried to run
me back. I...."

Something hard jabbed Culver in the spine. A low-
pitched voice sounded in his ear. "Steady, Bucko, and step
back here. Keep your hands up!"

The world was crashing about Culver's ears and he
cursed himself inwardly for taking anything for granted,
for becoming absorbed in the conversation within and
dropping his guard. An expert hand moved over his body
while the gun held hard against his back. He felt his own
gun slipped from its holster but he didn't dare make a play.
A man who has his back to an armed foe is outmaneuvered
before he starts.

"All right. Now turn around and give me a look at you!"

Culver turned slowly and cursed softly. The man who
had captured him was Bill Gregory. He might have figured
that they'd leave the driver outside for a lookout. Gregory

was grinning at him. A gesture commanded him away from the vicinity of the window. Gregory was having his minute and he proposed to enjoy it.

"So, it's smart-boy Culver?" he sneered. "Welcome to our city. Seems like somebody told me you were too bright for the dumb boys in the racket. Right?"

"I didn't say so, did I?"

"You got caught like a dumb flatfoot." There was a spiteful look of triumph on the gangster's face. "At that, I'm sorry for you. What you'll get when I bring you in will be huge."

He leaned forward. "I'd tell you to jump my gun and take it clean instead o' goin' in, only I wouldn't kill you. I'd just drop you. The boss wouldn't forgive me if I spoiled his fun."

Culver's eyes were level, his face expressionless. "Seems as though I remember you being a boss one time?" he said slowly. "The place was Kerry Patch or something like that, wasn't it?"

Gregory's eyes smoldered. "Never you mind that. I'm smarter than a lot of bosses in this town. What I started to tell you was what was going to happen to you." He stuck his jaw out. "Maybe you remember Matty Coyne. The boss pulled all o' his nice red hair out in little bunches with a pliers. He was bald-headed when he got the rest. Want me to tell you the rest?"

"Never mind, Bill. Mind if I take a smoke before you take me in?" Culver seemed suddenly to slump. The spirit went out of him. Bill Gregory grinned.

"Go ahead, but don't forget this gun, guy."

"I won't." Culver fished out a limp package and offered a smoke to his captor. Bill Gregory declined with a sly smile to reach for the package. Holding the gun steady, he brought forth a smoke from his own pocket. He was not worrying about weapons. He had frisked Culver carefully. Nor did Culver seem to be thinking of weapons. He was a slumped, dejected figure. Taking a cigar lighter from his vest pocket, he held it out.

INSTINCTIVELY, GREGORY leaned forward; then he started to draw back. He wasn't fast enough. There was a hissing sputter and a sharp report like the cracking of a dry twig. Bill Gregory gasped and reeled back on his heels. The gun roared. Culver side-stepped like a fighter at the moment that he pressed the tear gas cartridge release on the lighter. With a pantherish leap, he closed in to the left of the roaring gun. His right fist dropped and came up like a rocket. As it exploded against the gangster's jaw, he swept over with his left hand and wrenched the gun free. Blinded with gas and numbed by the blow, Bill Gregory plunged forward and fell face down on the ground.

Sounds of hurried movement came from the Mill. A man stood stupidly framed in the lighted window for a fraction of a second with a gun in his hand and Culver fired. The light went out and there was a whistling gasp from beyond the window. Culver faded out close to the ground. His lips tightened back over his teeth.

"Exit Monty Morello!" He muttered. "Next!"

The echo of his shot died and a smothering silence fell over the Cider Mill. Culver pressed his body close to the ground and waited. He heard a careful movement to his right, and his hand tightened on the trigger. Bill Gregory was climbing groggily to his feet.

Pawing at his eyes and rocking back on his heels like a punch-drunk pug, the gangster started to weave his unsteady way toward the doorway of the mill. Culver crawled quietly after him. Bill Gregory quite evidently was in a muddled frame of mind. He did not quite know what had happened to him, but there was some instinct operative in his mind that was urging him to seek the sanctuary of the mill. Culver sensed drama in that decision.

"Maybe he knows now why he isn't a big shot," he whispered. "Too much mouth. If he'd taken me in, instead of hanging around and making a damned barber out of himself, he'd have been a hero...."

Bill Gregory was facing the door now. He fumbled in his pocket for Culver's automatic, drew it, and started up the steps. Culver's eyes narrowed and he held his own weapon ready. "Cordo will figure that, since there was only one shot the first time and a damned hostile shot the next time, that anybody left out here is the enemy...."

Bill Gregory had reached the top step. He swayed there and his foot scraped the stone. The door opened with hair-raising suddenness and flame stabbed the darkness. There was a sharp report and Gregory stiffened to his full height. The man in the doorway fired again. As Gregory broke in two and slumped forward with his hands against his middle, Culver laid a bullet straight through the doorway.

He heard a strangled cry, the surprised, hurt cry of a man who considers himself victor only to find defeat and death reaching for him. The gun in the doorway spoke again and the flash came low, the bullet going off wild into the trees. The location of that flash told much. The man who was firing was falling as he fired.

Culver blazed another bullet across sill-high and shifted his position. The echoes boomed weirdly through the mill and tumbled off into silence. Culver wet his lips.

"That would be Hymie Katz! Cordo coming up...."

**HE COULD** not afford to make any mistakes now. Pete Cordo was plenty bad with the gun. He did not take part in gun battles while he had hired men handy, but he had held his own when he was coming up and he would be a dangerous article when cornered. As long as he holed up in that old stone fort, he'd be safe from a lone aggressor moving about in the darkness.

Culver frowned and then shrugged. "I'll take a chance that he won't dare shoot at a voice and that he wouldn't hit me if he did shoot at my voice."

Shifting toward the trees and the parked car, Culver sent a shout toward the Mill. "All right, you Cordo! Stay there. I'll be back with the boys...."

His shout woke more echoes but there was no reply from the Mill. Culver moved swiftly to the far side of the parked car. The keys were in the ignition and he set the switch. Then he sprawled along the running board and reached in until he could press the starter with his hand. The engine burst into song, full-throated and roaring. Almost at the same instant, there came a flash and a roar from the wing of the house closest to the car—then another and another and another.

It was good shooting and it riddled the spot where Culver would have been if he'd tried to drive the car away. Inflating his lungs, Culver gave a wild scream and, reaching into the car, pulled the throttle open wide. The fierce roar of a big eight turned full gun and racing shook the very trees. Culver smiled grimly and rolled off behind the car, crawling rapidly toward the mill once more.

To anybody willing to accept the evidence of his senses, it would appear that one of those viciously pumped bullets had killed the man in the car, and that he had fallen on the throttle. There was something horribly convincing about that roaring engine, something nerve destroying. Culver had to fight the insane impulse to go and turn the thing off himself. He did not think that Cordo could resist it.

Cordo didn't. He waited for a horrible three minutes of roaring sound and then he crept slowly from the mill, his gun in his hand. Culver recognized the unmistakable outline of that hulking form and his lips curled.

"The big shot himself—doing his thinking in person. If he had a brain, he'd turn Bridwell loose and make him investigate."

Carefully he stalked the crouching figure of the big gangster. The man was within ten paces of the car, when Culver materialized out of the shadows at his back. He had to shout to make his voice carry over the roar of horse-power rampant.

"Game's up, Cordo! Hoist 'em."

Pete Cordo bent at the knees and stiffened. He might have been a man straining to hear, a rabbit frightened half to death and hesitating on the verge of flight. Or a mad killer who hears the unwelcome sound of taps. For a second, he stood thus and then he whirled with tigerish speed, his gun coming up with flame coloring the muzzle.

**HIS LIPS** a thin line and his features frozen granite hard, Dean Culver stood with his feet firmly planted, waited a split second till his man had whirled completely around and then squeezed the trigger. He only fired once, but Pete Cordo's long arms were flung wildly as he completed his desperate spin, his gun fell from his hand as he collapsed. One shot had been plenty.

Dean Culver smiled a hard smile, and slowly removed his hat. He looked quizzically at the neat hole that had been drilled in his head-covering and ran his hand thoughtfully through his hair. He turned the body of Pete

Cordo over and exposed the wide, reddening stain on the man's chest.

"Anyway, Pete," he said quietly, "I didn't get you in the back. You went out pouring it...."

He turned soberly toward the house, suddenly conscious of an overwhelming sense of weariness. The past hour had been a terrific strain and killing depressed him, although he was not squeamish about gangsters. Since mobsters were so adept at giving it, it was his philosophy that they should expect to take it.

Still, there was something about snuffing a man that produced a wave of brain nausea. One didn't like to think of it too much.

Hymie Katz lay sprawled in the little hallway inside the door. Hymie was quite dead, and Culver did not go into any detailed examination beyond that. He switched on the light. Beau Bridwell looked up at him with wide eyes.

"Where—how did you get here, Culver?"

Culver produced a pen knife and carefully cut the little con's bonds. "I came out here, Bridwell, to hear you tell Pete Cordo what you wouldn't tell me...."

Bridwell's face whitened. "I... Culver, I wasn't holding out, honest to God. I did get those papers before the gang got there, but I was afraid to tell you. Doc Bromley up at the big house told me you were square, and that you'd help me if I was. Honest, Culver, I was afraid you wouldn't believe me about the murder if I admitted about those papers."

Culver looked into the man's faded eyes and saw earnestness there. He waved indifferently. "Okay, Bridwell. It turned out for the best anyway. I did you a dirty trick and used you for bait to get Pete Cordo out some place where I could work on him."

Bridwell swallowed hard. "He… that, is he?"

Culver nodded. "Yes," he said curtly. "He is."

## CHAPTER NINE
## WHO KILLED O'RYAN?

**I**T WAS quiet in the big room at the old Cider Mill, doubly quiet in the memory of booming guns that had awakened echoes just a few short minutes before. Beau Bridwell cleared his throat.

"There's another feller in there, Culver. Feller that Cordo brought out here when he brought me."

Culver stiffened. He shook his head, then his jaw snapped. He had forgotten Dick Harper. With a muttered curse, he rose, entered the other room, and cut the bonds from the securely tied and thoroughly scared mobster.

"You, Culver? What was…."

"Never mind. You don't have to know."

Culver herded his man savagely into the other room. Harper stopped short and Bridwell came to his feet with a sharp gasp. Bridwell broke the silence first.

"Dick Harper. How in hell?"

Culver frowned. This wasn't in his scenario. "Do you know this mutt, Bridwell?"

The query was inane, but Culver's brain was numb. Bridwell nodded. "I sure do. Dick used to be a competitor of mine. You remember, Culver, I told you that there were only a few fellers could open a can by listening to the tumblers and…."

A great weight dropped off Culver. He felt as though a wet sponge had been wiped across his brain. His jaw set hard and his eyes bored into Dick Harper's blotched face. "So that's the racket," he growled. "I wondered why Vito had you hanging around. You're the busy little can opener who gets dope out of other people's safes for Bart Brunderson, eh?"

Dick Harper cowered. He put up one shaking hand as though to protest, and stopped in mid-motion to rub his chin. Culver's eyes were gleaming. He whipped around once more to Beau Bridwell. "Look at him again, Bridwell. Look at him closely. Do you see anything else familiar about him besides the fact that you know him? Look, man?"

Beau Bridwell's lips trembled. "Why yes, I...."

Culver wheeled again. Harper seemed folding up in his tracks. Culver levelled a finger at him and his voice snapped like a whip lash. "You murdered Judge O'Ryan, you dirty mugg!"

"No. I never...."

"You lie. Spit it out quick." Culver had his automatic in his hands. Dick Harper trembled, then a crafty look came into his eyes.

"Yeah. I did it," he said. "I socked him with a hunk of pipe. Vito didn't let me have no gun because he'd kept me off the liquor, and he give me a shot o' coke instead, and he wouldn't let me have no gun, and me, I wouldn't go on any job without no weapon at all, and I dragged that hunk o' pipe."

**THE WORDS** were tumbling out now as though the man had been longing to claim the most sensational murder of the decade. Culver stopped him with one savage gesture. "What did you need a weapon for? Vito had a gun, didn't he? And Vito was along."

Dick Harper stepped right into the trap. "Sure. But that wasn't like me having a gun. Like I told you, Vito didn't let me have no gun. It was good I had that hunk o' pipe. Vito, he didn't have no guts when the old man come down. Me, I was the feller stood there and let him have it...."

"That's swell." Culver's lips twisted savagely. "You ought to get publicity on that, Dick. You must sit down and write it all out. NOW."

The crafty smile came back to Dick Harper's lips. "No, ain't dumb," he said. "I don't mind telling you fellers because you can't tell the cops after all this shooting around here."

Culver lighted a cigarette. "Something in that, Dick. Especially when Pete Cordo and Hymie Katz and Bill Gregory are lying around dead." His eyes narrowed. "But wouldn't it be terrible, Dick, if you got shot accidentally in the foot and left away out here with those corpses? Especially, Dick, if somebody tipped off some of Cordo's mob and sent them out here...."

The pallor in Dick Harper's face gave testimony of the fact that he was able to imagine some of the things that would happen. Culver took a notebook out of his pocket, tore out a half dozen sheets and flipped his fountain pen on the table beside them. "Get busy, Dick, and write. Be sure and mention Vito, too."

With a sob in his throat, Dick Harper wrote.

Three quarters of an hour later, Culver left Beau Bridwell in his own rooms on guard over a sullen prisoner who had been somewhat mollified by the gift of a quart of Scotch. Under the mattress in the same room, without Dick Harper being at all aware of it, there reposed the papers of Judge O'Ryan retrieved on the way from the tool shed behind his house.

"Bridwell," he said as he left, "watch that mugg close. One hour before you're scheduled to do what I told you to do, you let him loose."

"You mean free, altogether?" Bridwell was incredulous.

"Yeah. That's it. Let him roam."

With a casual wave, Dean Culver went down the hall. From a phone booth down stairs, he called the *Press-Courier*. When he came out, he was smiling grimly. The *Blue Barrel* had the front page again, but the fun was just starting. He was levelling down the sights at last at the man he wanted to get.

## CHAPTER TEN
## THE PAY-OFF

A THOUSAND passers-by might walk the narrow street on which the two story headquarters of Bart Brunderson stood, without noticing anything about the building except that the windows were dirty and that is was difficult to read the sign which carried the legend "Bartholomew Brunderson—Real Estate." To those in the know, the faded sign was no more important than the dirty windows. Bart Brunderson was in the real estate business only when the city was contemplating the purchase of land for some purpose. At such times, Black Bart always had advance information and options on the desired property snugly tucked away. His real estate profits on such deals were enormous, but they represented only a fraction of the business that he did in the shabby building.

It was dark outside when Dean Culver came to the building as a distant clock chimed the half hour after nine. There was light behind the dirty windows, however, and the sound of laughter came from within. Culver smiled and mounted the steps. He turned the knob of the front door and let himself into a semi-dark hallway. The voices in the big room off to the left hushed as his footsteps sounded. He turned toward the light and stepped into the room.

Black Bart was sitting with his face toward the door, but the eagerness of his expression faded into puzzled anger when he recognized the intruder. Vito Torino, whose chair had been tilted back against the wall, let his heels click on the floor. A dozen ward heelers, gangsters, and hangers-on looked at Culver as a wolf pack might look at a prospective victim. Culver removed his hat and brushed some imaginary dust from about the bullet hole in the alpine.

"Good evening, gentlemen," he said softly, "did I intrude on a meeting?"

Black Bart's eyes retreated behind the fatty pouches that hid them opportunely at times. He rolled a dead cigar the full length of his lips and back again. The mysterious taking off of Pete Cordo at about the hour that Culver had been scheduled to die was a blow to Bart Brunderson, and he had not yet figured it out. While the papers were busy laying the killing to a war with the Torino mob, Bart Brunderson knew differently. In a game where knowledge is power, he found himself suddenly without knowledge on a subject of importance. He had already played with the idea of making terms with Culver at almost any price. It wasn't a nice thought but it was preferable to the nasty question in Vito Torino's eyes. Culver's sudden appearance in this gathering called his hand. He had to be a friend or an enemy of Culver's and the mob was waiting for his decision. He shifted his body uncomfortably.

"How are you, Culver?" he compromised. "Want to sit around and wait for the cops?"

**CULVER RAISED** his eyes innocently, too innocently. "You haven't got anything to do with the cops, I hope?" His tone was mocking. Black Bart's eyes, hidden in the folds of fat, had been sizing up the room. The wolves were hostile to Culver, definitely hostile—and this time the lead wolf had to run with the pack. He couldn't risk a challenge of his leadership. Too many things had gone wrong lately. His lips curled.

"Culver," he growled. "You don't fool me a bit. I told you before and I'm telling you again that I hate your guts. You ain't regular. That crack I made about the cops was sarcasm, see? Scram. I figured you for a stool, see."

The pack was leaning forward now, applauding silently. Culver blew on his hat and quietly replaced it. He was looking calmly at Bart Brunderson but his attention was on the little office off in the corner; the office which opened on the areaway and that was separated from this room by a thin partition. That office wasn't important normally; it was a blind and a shabby pretense of a place where nothing important was kept. Tonight it was very important. Culver yawned.

"I'm disappointed, Brunderson," he said, "to find you in such bum humor. You were laughing when I came in. You wouldn't be worried about a sucker you framed off the press would you?"

He looked around the room as he spoke. Anything to keep their attention for a while. Brunderson paled. He was conscious of something under the surface and he was suddenly alarmed. He had been confidently waiting for his laugh on the District Attorney. Now some sense told him that Culver was connected with that joke of his somehow and that it might possibly turn out wrong. His coarse features worked.

"You're damned right," he snarled viciously. "I had you kicked off the sheets and I can brush you aside again if you get in my way; anything from picking pockets to murder— I'll hang it on you and make it stick. Now, get the hell out of here!"

He stood up as he spoke and there was a general tensing. Culver felt a tightening along his own spine. Time was his enemy and he had to whip Time into submission, stall, hold this crowd. He ignored the damning admission that had caused specks of red to dance before his eyes. He held his voice down, his features rigid.

"Would you like to know, Brunderson," he asked quietly, "just what happened to Pete Cordo and why?"

Black Bart's jaw dropped and a sibilant hiss ran around the room. Culver knew that he could commit suicide very easily in the next few minutes, but he remembered, too, that this crowd was waiting for a raid. They'd be careful here. Vito Torino was on his feet, his dark eyes flashing.

"What you know about the Cordo bump?" he challenged.

Culver shrugged. "I know you didn't do it, Vito," he said. "I got a tip that Pete was rubbed out because he was after the O'Ryan papers. I don't know."

THERE WAS no need for artificial means of holding this crowd's attention now. They would not have heard a trap drum in the little room beyond the partition. Black Bart was gripping the back of his chair.

"Who—who did it?" he gasped.

Culver made a gesture of bewilderment. "I don't know," he said, "but I got a phone call...."

He stopped there. Someone was whistling "After the Ball Was Over" out on the street. It was his signal. Culver relaxed and lighted a cigarette. His job was done. The crowd was shooting questions in machine gun fashion. Culver raised his hands.

"Hell, I can't answer all those. I thought Brunderson might know who wanted those papers and that he'd be able to tell who killed Pete Cordo."

"But why did anyone call you?" A ward boss threw the question from the corner of the room. Culver looked grave.

"There was a rumor out that Pete was going to have me bumped. This guy on the phone was friendly. He thought if I knew that Pete was going after those papers that I'd maybe rig a deal to work with him."

A whistle shrilled out in the street. Culver sat back in his chair and every eye turned to the door. Black Bart, master of himself for the moment, rose to his feet. A tramp of feet sounded in the hall and the frail figure of J. Gordon Joyce stood framed in the doorway. With a dramatic gesture, the District Attorney waved a paper.

"Brunderson," he shrilled, "I have a warrant to search...."

Black Bart laughed. "Search away, my hearty. Good luck to you."

Pale, uncertain and patently shaking, J. Gordon Joyce waved the police to their task. He had been talked into making this raid and he was trembling inside. They made quick work of the room in which the meeting was held and moved on the private office. Brunderson crowded in with them. Culver stood in the doorway. He could feel the pressure of the crowd at his back and he politely made room for Vito Torino, ushering him well up front.

Half-heartedly, the police started to turn out drawers while Bart Brunderson stood with his thumbs hooked in his suspenders and kidded them. "If you'll tell me what you're looking for, I'll help," he jeered.

J. Gordon Joyce crossed to the safe and gave the dial a turn. He had been told to do that, too, and he did it without confidence. The door opened and Bart Brunderson's jests died on his lips. He stiffened. The District Attorney reached inside the safe and pulled out a thick sheaf of papers. He gave a grunt of satisfaction. His eyes raised accusingly to Black Bart.

"These papers, Mr. Brunderson," he said coldly, "are the private papers of Judge O'Ryan; the evidence which he collected to show that you—and not Governor Barker— were the inspiration of graft and corruption in this city."

**THE CROWD** behind Culver was moving restlessly and Culver could almost hear the thought-wheels whir. He had planted an idea and these men were sure now that Torino's gang had killed Cordo for these very papers. If they hadn't, why hadn't Brunderson admitted having them?

Black Bart was white and he was leaning heavily against the wall. "I've been framed," he yelled. "It's a dirty frame. It won't hold up in court...."

"Oh, yes, it will." The District Attorney's voice was cold steel. "Do you think that you—with your reputation—can convict me of crooked methods? This, Man, is evidence."

He drew a sharp breath and literally hurled his next verbal bombshell. "Moreover," he said, "we have the murderer of Judge O'Ryan, self-confessed, at head-quarters with a full confession of his accomplice and... Stop him!"

Vito Torino turned to flee and a heavy-handed cop caught him and swung him around. He snarled at Black Bart. "Wise guy," he shouted. "Wise guy, ain't you...."

The rest was silenced as he was bundled out of the room. Black Bart rode with him in the hurry wagon.

Out on the sidewalk before the grimy building that had been the Brunderson nest of corruption for so long, Dean Culver stood with his hands in his pockets. "Pete Cordo died with a gun in his fist," he murmured, "and Black Bart hollers 'frame.' Some smart egg wrote once that 'they die by the sword who live by the sword' and ain't it the truth? Maybe it was dirty to have Beau Bridwell tap that can and plant the evidence, but how can you get rid of a dirty framer unless you frame him? The answer is that you can't."

The crowd had scattered to spread the word through the underworld where each man would interpret the facts according to his lights. Some would read into Brunderson's possession of the papers a link with the killing of Pete Cordo; other, more thoughtful souls, would smell a frame-up and pay off silently on a new force in the field of crime, an unseen worker behind the scenes who had been big enough to make a sucker out of Black Bart.

Dean Culver turned back to the deserted office. Over Bart Brunderson's own phone, he called Joe Loftus, City Editor of the *Press-Courier*. Culver had spent four and a half hours when he was loggy for sleep in copying the important papers of the O'Ryan collection. Those papers, with a pre-written story had gone to Loftus by special messenger just before Culver entered Brunderson's.

"*Blue Barrel*," he snapped. "The story goes as you've got it. Everything clicked like a puzzle. Perfect. Shoot it and— wait a minute!" A smile creased his hard features. "Bart Brunderson offered five grand for the killers of the Judge," he said slowly. "It was just a gesture, but he ought to pay for bum gestures. Collect it for me."

**HE TURNED** from the phone. Outside there was an off-key whistler rendering the dolorous strains of "After the Ball Was Over." Culver went out to meet Beau Bridwell and, for the first time, he shook hands with him.

"You're clear, Old Timer," he said, "and the governor's clear, and the only people who are hurt are people who had it coming." His eyes warmed. "You did one whale of a fast job on that safe. Great. I'm going to see that you get a stake."

Bridwell stammered, his pale eyes glowing. "Aw, that can was pie," he said. "Kids in short pants was opening that kind when I was in my prime...."

Culver was frowning with a sudden recollection. "Tell me something," he said. "Why in blazes did you climb out an upstairs window at O'Ryan's when it was easier to get out downstairs? I can't figure that play if you did it."

The look of awe which was habitually on Beau Bridwell's face when he looked at Dean Culver faded. His chest swelled with the pride of a vindicated old timer who knows his ropes.

"Anybody ought to figure that," he said condescendingly. "Those other guys came in after me, didn't they? They used my entry, didn't they? Hell's Bells! Was I going to walk out into the arms or their lookout?"

A sheepish smile crossed Culver's face. "And I was just thinking that I was smart," he said. "Well that just goes to show something or another. Shut up about it, Bridwell, and I'll buy you a drink."

Together they went to Big John Zorro's.

# THE BLUE BARREL

NO ONE CALLED DEAN CULVER
THE BLUE BARREL—FOR NO ONE
KNEW HE WAS THE AUTHOR
OF THE UNDERWORLD-GOSSIP
COLUMN SIGNED WITH THAT
NAME EACH NIGHT IN THE STAR.
IF THE EASY-MONEY PLAYERS
HAD EVER GUESSED THAT THE
MAN WHO PAID THEM OFF AT THE
TWIN MOONS WAS THE WALTER
WINCHELL OF THE OTHER SIDE
OF THE LAW, HE'D HE CASHING IN
HIS OWN CHECKS AT THE FIRST
TURN OF THE WHEEL, INSTEAD
OF THOSE OF THE GAMBLERS HE
SPUN IT FOR.

**D**EAN CULVER sat behind the spinning wheel and the clicking ball at the big table in the Twin Moons and no one noticed him. Before him nightly there passed the parade of plungers, chiselers, big shots and suckers that swell the human tide of a big-time gambling-house and into his ears there passed the gossip, the rumor and the stark staring truth about the human undertow.

There were at least three men in the room right now who would have killed Dean Culver without a qualm if they knew their man, and fifty or more at large in the city who would have helped them; not counting those in the big house who couldn't help, nor those who would have turned over in their graves if Culver stepped on the sod above them.

The human tide ebbed and flowed and Culver sat impassive with the tiny rake in his hand, the stacks of chips before him and the green eyeshade pulled low. He was the man that nobody noticed, the croupier, the dealer of roulette; hired man for the Goddess of Chance.

But Dean Culver was also the *Blue Barrel*.

The bulldog edition of the *Morning Star* had just hit the street and from immaculate tables in the best hotels to the cracked counters of the greasy spoons, eyes were eagerly scanning the leaded type of the *Blue Barrel*. What Walter

Winchell had done for Broadway, the *Blue Barrel* was doing for the underworld, the half-fringe and the indiscreet circle of society that refuses to stay where it belongs. Above the column was a line-drawing cut of the weapon from which the column got its name; a savage-looking automatic with a thin wisp of smoke drifting from the muzzle.

The column, too, laid chiselers and double-crossers low, beside passing on the items that were hot news to those who read it. Tonight there was a typical item that named no names for those who were not in the know, but that identified the man mentioned by one significant word for those who did know him.

> The toughest hard-times streak in the history of local put-and-take parlors broke Tuesday night and is still breaking. The hard-times champ is gathering to himself a load of roulettuce while the moons shine....

The casual reader got nothing out of that except some doubtful slang and the glow that comes from knowing that somewhere a hard-luck streak has broken. To a great many people, however, there came a great urge to head for the Twin Moons in the hope that they might see the climax of another dramatic attempt to "break the bank at Monte Carlo."

**CULVER SAT** in the middle of the excitement with his face impassive and emotionless. Across from him sat Dan "Hard-times" Healy who was still riding his streak behind a staggering stack of chips; a middle-aged man whose forehead was lost in a great bald expanse of skull, and whose quizzical gray eyes, level through years of all varieties of hard luck, were level still.

"Twenty-three on the black."

The crowd gasped as 23 came up for the fourth time in fifteen minutes, with Healy pulling in an enormous pile of blues. Healy had been on 23 every time that it had hit and he'd been off it when it missed. There was something uncanny about that to the spectators but Culver was unimpressed; outwardly or inwardly. Things like that happened when a man was hot and they didn't call for a logical explanation any more than did the fact that the ball never stopped in 23 when the man who played it was not hot. Streaks came and went but men didn't change very much. A man was fundamentally lucky or he wasn't. It had taken Dan Healy years to win the nickname of Hard-times Healy; he wouldn't lose it overnight— nor overcome the effect of those years either.

"Twenty-seven!"

Healy collected a small bet on the red and Paul Berlanger, the big, florid, double-chinned man on his left, cursed bitterly with no regard for the women in the gallery.

"Seventeen hasn't hit tonight," he complained.

Culver was raking the Berlanger chips off 17. Berlanger was as good an example as Healy for a book on luck. Berlanger was fundamentally lucky and streaks such as he had been having lately didn't change the fact. The man had been born with a diamond-studded gold spoon in his mouth and with a satchel full of good rubber-company stock in each fist. He had set a record for expensive idleness ever since, and he had never cared sufficiently for anyone but himself to be seriously hurt by the march of events.

"I'll take over, Culver."

It was his relief and Dean Culver slid out of his place to permit Larry Dane a spot behind the wheel. Few people noted the change. The wheel kept spinning no matter who the croupier. As he passed the check-girl on his way to the Twin Moons dining-room, Culver picked up his regular copy of the *Star*. It was left for him every night and, like most of the other regulars, he turned to page three and the *Blue Barrel*. He was reading it with a coolly critical eye when Healy, Paul Berlanger, a couple of hangers-on and three girls passed on the way to the big center table. Healy waved one plump hand.

"Couldn't do business without you, son," he said genially, "Thought it was time to lay off—"

He was past before Culver could answer and Culver didn't try. Nobody else in the party had given him so much as a nod but their voices reached him clearly. None of them was the soft-spoken type. Berlanger had folded back a copy of the *Star*. One of the others had the *Blue Barrel* already turned up. He showed it to Healy. Healy swore goodnaturedly.

"That 'hard-times' phrase instead of hard-luck is the tip-off," he said. "I'll have every moocher in town after me for a touch."

"The bird that writes that column is going to be found in an alley some day." The man who had presented the paper looked hard. "You might be maybe annoyed but some guys have been plumb ruined by things he prints."

Healy accepted a menu from the hovering waiter. "Nobody that I could ever worry about was ruined by it," he growled. "Mostly chiselers and muggs and double-crossers and—"

He was interrupted by a roar from Berlanger. "Listen to this! Just listen. I'm going to sue the hell out of this sheet if it's the last thing I ever do."

Healy collected a small bet on the red.

Sputtering with wrath, the big man stopped all conversation within range of his voice as he read the *Blue Barrel's* second-to-the-last paragraph aloud.

"The rubber industry has made a lot of millionaires but none of them left any formulas for stretching ordinary money as one of the heirs is finding out. Said heir had better get busy right away, too, on a formula of his own for taking the bounce out of rubber checks… too many of his have bounced right out of the banks they were written on… and good nature doesn't always stretch, either."

**DEAD, STRICKEN** silence greeted the reading. One of the hangers-on rubbed his chin and looked at Berlanger furtively. He knew as the others did that Paul Berlanger had inherited the Berlanger balloon fortune which had had the taint of World War profiteering on it before he got it, and that had nothing constructive associated with it since he inherited. The spots has been wondering for years how deep the Berlanger pocket-book actually was.

"Maybe the guy didn't mean you...." The hanger-on seemed to realize that that would have been better unsaid. Berlanger's narrow eyes glared at him and one ponderous fist hit the table.

"Me? Of course, he can't mean me. That's the poison of it. People who don't know any better will think so. That item is going to hurt me...."

Hard-times Healy was looking across the table thoughtfully. "You're just calling attention to it, Paul," he said. "Ignore the damned thing. Let's order—"

Culver had not looked up but he had heard every word and a faint smile curled the corner of his lips. Fatty Berlanger had had his cake. And he'd eaten it. And it was a darned late day for Berlanger to start worrying about his honor or his reputation.

Upstairs in the safe of the Twin Moons there was about five thousand dollars in checks of Berlanger rubber that were guaranteed to bounce out of any bank—and the Twin Moons was only one bright spot in the far-flung night-life lines. It amused Culver to imagine the reaction of Berlanger if the man knew how close he was to the *Blue Barrel* in person!

It mightn't be very amusing at that.

By the time that Culver had finished his dessert and coffee, gaiety had returned to the big table. Culver didn't look toward it as he rose from his place. It was bound to be gay. Healy had taken nearly thirty grand away from the Twin Moons tonight alone. There were only two places in the city that could stand a tap like that and the Two Moons couldn't stand many more like it.

Dollar Hanlon was standing in the foyer when Culver came out. Hanlon ran the Twin Moons, owned most of it and played the game on the square. He knew a lot about Culver that nobody else knew and he still trusted him; if he suspected more than he knew, he kept his mouth shut.

"Healy's carrying the big kick," he said, "and he's tired. He's not going back to the big room. He's going to shake those chirpers and go home."

Culver nodded. "You want me to go along."

"Exactly. And listen, Culver—"

"Yes."

"You're hard-shelled and you don't believe in luck. I'm just as hard and I do. It just ain't in the record of a guy like Healy that he should spend big dough. A guy with luck like his always draws kings against aces when it looks like he's doing all right."

"What about it?"

"Just watch yourself! Watch him, too. He's a good guy and, if he wasn't, we got to think of ourselves. Anybody that wins big sugar here has to get home with it."

"They always have." Culver's tone was curt.

Hanlon turned away. "Yeah," he said. "They always have."

Culver lighted a cigarette, looked thoughtfully at the flame and moved toward the phone booths in the alcove. He'd anticipated this job because he'd done others like it but he wasn't going to enjoy himself. Big winners were always escorted home from the Twin Moons and the job often fell to Culver. Dollar Hanlon covered gentlemen with gentlemen rather than with hoods and Dean Culver was a gentleman from away back; he just happened to be a gentleman who was also handy with a gun. He entered the booth and dialed a number. When a girl answered, his voice deepened and he asked for the city editor.

"Randall? *Blue Barrel*. Get this. I've got the low-down on the Smoky Kendall kill. Run it 'flash' on top of the column like this: 'The poultry racketeer who was foully murdered in the park the other night did not blink out in a gang feud. He got the curtain call because his playfellows suspected him of being a see-man for the G-men.'"

Culver hung up and turned away. It was a nice item on a case that was being headlined with bad guesses. He'd got it by listening when he could have been talking. He shook the ash from his cigarette, then stiffened. The door of the other booth banged open and he almost slammed into the big figure that erupted. He cursed his own carelessness for not hearing the man come in and raised his eyes to the other's hot stare.

The man was Paul Berlanger.

For a moment there was something like fear in the big man's eyes; then a look almost of triumph. Culver nodded indifferently as one nods to a casual acquaintance. Berlanger didn't return the nod but Culver felt the man's eyes on his back as he went toward the foyer. He shrugged his shoulders impatiently.

He was no longer playing with the idea of what Berlanger would look like if Berlanger knew that he was the *Blue Barrel*; he was wondering now *if* he knew.

**HARD-TIMES HEALY** was waiting; a blocky man whose well worn topcoat took the edge of elegance off his evening attire. He was smoking a cigar and he was alone. He was generally alone. He'd lost a wife and three sons in four separate accidents and several fortunes in bank failures. His weakness was neither women nor liquor; merely cards and roulette.

"H'areya, boy! All set to lead me by the hand past all the bad, bad wolves?"

Culver grinned. "You made it lots of times without me."

"Never with money. Not out of here." Healy shifted his cigar and looked at his watch. "We'll go in Berlanger's car," he said. "I've got to stop at his place for a minute. Matter of business—"

"No dice." Culver shook his head. "I take the responsibility and I see you right home—my way."

Healy looked at him. "That way, huh." He shifted the cigar again. "Berlanger will be alone, kid," he said. "I owe him favors. His chauffeur' and the servants have the night out. We'll take his car from his place to mine by ourselves. I pretty nearly have to do it that way."

Culver frowned. That servant gag, of course, was Berlanger's. Maybe Healy believed it, maybe not. It was one of the things that made Berlanger a mugg. He'd kept his staff as long as he could—and all of them were trying to collect their salaries while Berlanger continued to play the gay-boy of the hot spots on the proceeds of his no-bank play money. If the big slob had ever done favors for Healy, he'd done them as he did everything else; publicly and with a nourish that would advertise his own great-heartedness. Still—

Healy was chewing the cigar. "It's either that, kid, or I sign a waiver of protection with Hanlon and you don't go."

Culver made up his mind between the two motions of a shrug. "I might come in handy," he said.

Berlanger appeared with a showy blonde draped on his arm. He was patting her hand and he ignored Culver who had started over to the checkroom for his topcoat. There was a white-tie-and-ermine group of late arrivals who had just recognized the notorious Berlanger and were whispering about him. Berlanger changed his course to pass close to them and patted the blonde's hand again.

"Tomorrow at Audrey's," he said. And his voice made no secret of it. Audrey's was a spot where men bought things for women and where the mention of price was as vulgar as the payment of a price was necessary.

"Sorry if I kept you waiting, old chap." Berlanger's voice was full of the old arrogant patronage as he steamed up to Healy. Culver trailed along unnoticed. The car was in a no-parking zone three doors up the block. Berlanger tore up the ticket that was on it and slid under the wheel.

"Rather an adventure to drive my own car for a change," he drawled. Culver lighted a cigarette. Berlanger had been having that sort of an adventure for over a week. Culver, alone in the back seat of the sedan, did not talk. It was not his business to; he was a human machine again, a man with a blue-barreled gun instead of a man with a little rake.

**HE WAS** still a machine when they entered Berlanger's bachelor bungalow behind Berlanger's key, but he dropped the role when Berlanger stopped before the sliding doors that led to his private study off the library and still ignoring Culver's presence, addressed himself directly to Healy.

"We can speak in here *privately*," he said.

Culver stiffened and, ignoring Berlanger as completely as the man had ignored him, held out his hand to Healy. "If I'm still responsible," he said, "you can give me your stake to take care of; if I'm not, you can shake hands and I'll get out of here."

"You mean to insinuate—" Berlanger was aware of him now, bristling.

Healy looked pained. "Hell, boy, I'd trust you with more than that but I'm not going to give it to you for personal reasons. I'd like you to—"

Culver shook hands with him. "Goodnight, then," he said.

He was on his heel and headed for the door, cursing himself inwardly as a fool but heading away just the same. He'd had enough of Berlanger and the high hand-shake and the royal razoo. The man had brought Healy out here to make a touch on the strength of past favors and that, of course, was why Healy was hanging on to the poke. Well, let Healy stomach the big slob; he didn't have to.

Culver was blazing mad inside. Some wary monitor kept warning him that he was not his own man right now; he had taken a job and all that went with it and he was walking out on it for personal reasons. He could hear Dollar Hanlon's gruff voice again.

"You don't believe in luck... I do.... We got ourselves to think about...."

The phrases were a ding-dong insistent chorus by the time that he reached the sidewalk and he stopped. The house was dark except for a weak lamp in the hallway and the lights behind the drawn shades of the study. He lit a cigarette, cursed.

"I'll swallow it," he growled. "Healy is a good guy. But I'll wait here. I'd have been on the outside anyway."

He took a half-turn, then flinched instinctively and dropped his right shoulder low. Somewhere in the house a heavy-caliber gun boomed and three sharp banging sounds were all but swallowed up in the echo.

Culver went in, charging. He was conscious of Berlanger's hoarse bellow which had sounded on the heels of the shot and of the fact that the man was calling out now as though for help. The fact that it was Berlanger's voice—and not Healy's—chilled him. After all, there had been a shot.

His worst fears were confirmed. Just inside the door to Berlanger's private study, Dan Healy lay face down. One arm was crumpled under him and the other stretched out, fingers curved talon-fashion, as though, dying, he had striven to crawl toward Berlanger's big desk which was broadside to the open window. Berlanger was making gobbling sounds in his throat and waving his hands, but Culver dropped on one knee beside Healy.

This time the hard-times streak was definitely over.

The bullet had caught him squarely in the forehead and the eyes were glazed now and hazed with blood. Culver straightened, his body taut.

Berlanger seemed to be finding his voice. One of his waving hands held a gun but he was not pointing it. "Stick-up," he rasped. "Fellow came in the window, took all our money, Healy tried to jump him—"

"Yeah? I'll look at your gun." Culver's lips were a thin line. He had not made a motion toward his own armpit, but his eyes were narrowed and his hands were in the clear. Berlanger sneered and the panic seemed to drop away from him. He presented the weapon butt-first. It was a Smith & Wesson revolver, .38 caliber, and it took only a glance to show that it had not been recently fired.

"Satisfied, wise guy?" Berlanger's thick lips curled. "It hasn't been fired, has it?"

"Maybe it should have been." Culver moved to the window and looked out. The two front windows were closed and he had never been out of sight of them himself. This one opened out on a side porch that was screened by dense vines trained along a wire network except on the side toward the rear of the house. A man could have run that way or a gun could have been thrown that way; but a man would leave tracks and a gun could be found. He didn't know if there were either tracks or gun out there, but that could be found out. He turned back into the room. Berlanger's face was grim, his fleshy jaw hard.

"How did you mean that last crack?"

"The way it fell. You had a gun. If there was another fellow, why did he do all the shooting?"

"I wasn't the gunman hired to protect Dan Healy."

IT WAS a straight, hard shot. Culver took it without blinking but it hit home. He was in a bad spot. At its best, his story of his reasons for walking out was bad; but Berlanger's story could not be expected now to substantiate his and Dan Healy couldn't talk. He'd been framed once before by just such a slob as this and his nostrils were sniffing danger. He met it head-on, his stare hard on Berlanger.

"Suppose we let the cops find out if there was another man in this." He moved toward the phone on the desk. Berlanger rested his shoulders against the wall. He had never once shown an interest in the fate of Healy nor in the sprawled body on the floor.

"If there wasn't another man, there'd be a gun," he said. "Suppose you find one, Sherlock."

Something in his tone stopped Culver in the act of reaching for the phone. The man was too sure of that touch about the missing gun, too try-and-prove-it in his general attitude. He'd be different, of course, when the cops came; the "sorrowing friend" probably. Right now he was being himself and Culver knew this man's gambling habits well. Paul Berlanger was a system player, not a player of long shots.

He knew instinctively now that the police would not find a gun. He didn't know why they wouldn't, but he knew.

Dan Healy was on the floor, shot to death. His money, no doubt, was gone. His dear friend, Paul Berlanger, would be grief-stricken and the only witness. There would be no gun and Dean Culver, the man assigned to protect Dan Healy, would have no story that would stand up anywhere. After that, there would be the digging up of skeletons and Culver's old record would dangle before the public.

Berlanger's smile was hard, tight. "The money is gone, too," he said viciously. "Maybe you know something about that. You tried to get your hands on it before—"

Culver grunted. So that was the way that the story shaped! "O.K.," he said grimly. "The gun and money are not in the room. I'll take your word for that. I won't take your word that a man took them out." He passed up the desk and the telephone, moving once more to the window. He was remembering the banging sounds that had followed almost immediately upon the report of the gun.

He looked out of the window this time with an eye to detail.

The porch was dark and it angled around the front of the building; screened thickly with vines run on wire the whole way. A man who plunged through that window and turned to the right would have crossed the path of Culver inevitably as Culver ran back into the house. Going the other way, he would have run ten yards at least over a cement walk before he could get clear of a hedge fence into the grounds—or continued on another ten yards to a high picket fence.

Culver shook his head, stiffened. His hand had brushed a hook screwed into the wood of the sill; a strong hook of the kind that is used to hang hammocks.

"Seen enough?"

The new note in Berlanger's voice brought him around fast. The man was sneering at him and the gun was no longer being waved around vaguely as an accessory to a lot of gestures. It was pointed squarely now at Culver's belt line. Culver eyed the gun, lifted his eyes to Berlanger.

"That doesn't buy you a thing," he said grimly. "A second kill would just make it twice as hard for you to wiggle out."

**BERLANGER CHUCKLED.** The triumphant mood of the super-egotist, proud of his own planning, was coming back to him. "What I need," he said bluntly, "is a fugitive to make the tracks that a man with a gun would make. This play-acting has gone far enough. I kept it up only while there was a chance of some yokel being attracted by the shot. You, my jail-bird friend, are going to be the fugitive...."

Culver's face didn't change expression. He might have been Fortune's hired man still, dealing wealth or disaster from behind a clicking ball, for all of the emotion that he showed. Inwardly, he was rocked. There had been a chance that Berlanger had heard his telephone call and knew him for the *Blue Barrel;* that had worried him. He had not suspected this. Berlanger's face was like wet plaster with the strain that was on him, but there was a sneer on his lips, a chuckle in his throat.

"Surprised you, didn't I? Well, I've made it my business lately to find out such things about men who handle money—or protect it. You see the spot you're in?"

Culver did see. It was true, of course. He'd done a rap in Illinois. He'd been a crack newspaperman in Chicago until the blow-off in the Lingle murder case gave some big shots the idea that newspapermen could be made fall guys for a lot of things. Culver had been the horrible example and he'd stepped into a frame while chasing crime news; a frame so perfect that his own paper believed it. The jury was a cinch with memories of the Lingle "exposé" still fresh. Culver had taken the rap standing up.

He'd become the *Blue Barrel* since he came out and a lot of framers, chiselers and double-crossers had bitten the dust. He wouldn't stand a chance with his record, with his present job as employee of a gambling house and with the prestige of the Berlanger name against him. It was almost as neat as the last frame that he'd stepped into. Berlanger held the gun steady.

"All I know," he said, "when the cops come, is that a lone gunman stuck us up and shot Healy, that he took nothing of yours and that you made no effort to either stop him or pursue him. Naturally, after that, I held you for the police...."

Culver shrugged. "I know a box when I see one. What's the out?"

"Now you're talking sense. You just take it on the lam. I'll give you a head start and then call the cops. The rest depends on your luck. Stick around here and you won't have any luck."

Culver almost laughed aloud. It was fantastic that a thing like this could happen to anybody, but experience had taught him that even worse things happened. The weight of a prominent man's testimony against a man with a record was insupportable. Berlanger's associates might know that he was a heel but once he became a state's witness, nobody would be allowed to tell that to a jury.

"I'll take the lam," he said. "It's a better bet."

**THE GROUNDS** were dark and Culver faded into them like a shadow losing itself in shadow. He did not have his ears cocked for sirens because he did not expect any for a while. He believed that Berlanger would take his time about calling the cops; not because Berlanger would respect his word to Culver but because it would serve his purpose best to delay.

Right now Berlanger would be changing his story; eliminating the accomplice and putting the entire blame for the shooting of Healy upon Culver whose flight proved it. He wouldn't have forced Culver to take the lam if there hadn't been a weakness in the frame-up that he'd hung so neatly around Culver's neck. And Culver wouldn't have taken the lamister as the way out if he hadn't suspected that that weakness existed.

A gun and thirty thousand dollars didn't vanish without a trace in the time that it takes a gunshot echo to die.

Culver was circling back to the house; coming in from the front but hugging the shadows low down and with his eye on the porch. That porch was a regular cage for a man inside the vines and the wire network that supported them; but it was a ladder to the second floor for a man outside. He'd thought of that.

He moved in on them silently, tested them and went up softly. The porch roof was sloping and a trifle slippery but he clung to it and worked his way to the edge, above the window to Berlanger's study. There was a room directly above the study that opened out on the porch roof and it was closed. Beyond the edge of the roof and on an angle away from the study window was another second-story window that was open.

Culver smiled grimly and measured the distance to the sill from the edge of the porch. It was only a moderate jump for a man in condition but he wasn't worrying about the jump; he was worrying about making the jump to the sill, vaulting into the room and still retaining a hand free for his gun. That couldn't be done.

He moved over to the closed window but, as he suspected, that window was not only closed but locked. Under normal circumstances that wouldn't have worried him a lot; but it was no time or place for jimmy-work now. Any bit of business like that around a murder job could be juggled into evidence and confuse the issue. He went back to the porch edge. He looked at the narrow sill with distaste, shrugged—and took the jump.

His hands took the sill with a sure touch and he went into the room with a vaulting follow-through on his jump momentum. Paul Berlanger spun around from a bent position before a cabinet on the far side of the room and came up with his gun leveled.

Culver's hand moved toward his armpit and stopped. "So what?" he said.

Berlanger was shaken. He gripped the cabinet with one hand to steady himself and he remained in his crouch. His grip on the gun, however, was firm; the grip of grim determination. When he recognized Culver, the palsey left him. "You!"

There was puzzled wonder struggling with relief in his voice. He drew his body up so that his bulk concealed all except the general contour of the cabinet. Culver was eyeing him coldly.

"Sure, me! You needed a fugitive to put yourself in the clear; I needed a gun to clear myself. It looks like my pot."

"You're crazy."

"Yeah?" Culver eyed the gun in Berlanger's hand. It was the same one that he had looked at before and it was not the murder gun. Still it was a gun in the hand of a man who had committed murder.

"When I saw that hook on the sill and remembered how your family made its money," he said, "I knew how the gun and the money could have gone out of that room. When I climbed up on top of the porch and saw this open window, I knew where they could have gone. When I found you up here I knew I'd found them."

BERLANGER'S FINGER went white on the trigger and Culver, too far across the room to hope to jump successfully, tensed anyway; then Berlanger laughed. "A pipe dream. You're—"

Culver's eyes narrowed. "And when the cops come," he said, "perhaps you'll let them open that cabinet and look at the big rubber band fastened inside—"

Berlanger didn't shoot. He came across the room like a charging rhino, the gun held forward. Culver didn't draw and he didn't have time to duck before the avalanche was on him. He lashed out twice with his left hand, missed his grab for the menacing gunhand and brought Berlanger to his senses with a ploughing right that landed just above the belt.

The big man reeled back with the gun just out of Culver's reach; his left hand stabbing. "I'll shoot if you take another step."

There was panting hatred in it and Culver believed him. A man in Berlanger's fix didn't have a lot to lose. Berlanger was backing at an angle away from the cabinet.

"You're right," he said. "The gun's in there. In a bag with the money. It ought to have your fingerprints on it. Take it out."

Culver smiled and moved on the cabinet. It had double doors that opened out and they were hard to open. Once he had one side open, he had to wedge his body against it to keep it open. Strong rubber bands were fastened to each door-half. Inside there was an ingenious cage in which a canvas sack was neatly cradled. Culver saluted the ingenuity of the man who had devised it.

The cage was funnel-shaped and had, obviously, been fitted into the two halves of the cabinet door to keep them open against the pull of the bands. The wide end of the funnel had faced the open window and a long and powerful rubber band had been drawn through the hole in the funnel from a ring in the back of the cabinet. This band had been drawn down to the floor below and fastened to the hook outside the Berlanger study window with a canvas sack on the end of it. It had been ready for the first man with money whom Berlanger could entice into that room.

All that Berlanger had to do was hold Healy up, get his money and shoot him. While Healy's body was falling, he was able to whirl to the window, toss gun and money into the sack—then slide the sack off the hook.

The snap-back of that band had taken it right back to the ring in the back of the cabinet upstairs, and as it slammed through the funnel-like cage, it had taken the device right in with it; permitting the cabinet doors to close. Who would search for a layout like that?

Culver picked up the sack and held it in his hand. He raised his eyes to Berlanger. "What a fool you'd be," he said softly, "to let me get my hand on a gun even with the drop you've got."

Berlanger hesitated. There were greasy beads of sweat on his white face.

"Let me worry," he said. "Get that gun out!"

Culver let the sack dangle in his right hand and reached with his left. "And what a fool I'd be to fumble in a sack for a gun!"

His right hand snapped with the sudden fury of a tree that snaps back against a let-up in a high wind. Berlanger had been too intent upon one thing and the weighted sack caught him like a sandbag.

There was a thundering boom as his gun spoke, plaster cascaded from the wall and Culver leaped in behind the sack. His own gun jumped into his hand and he clubbed Berlanger's wrist as he charged. The big man's gun thudded against the floor and Berlanger sank after it on one knee. He was holding his wrist with one hand.

"Wait, Culver... Wait!" he said. "I'll treat you right. Half the cash if you'll back my story. More when I get on my feet. I was broke, desperate...."

Culver's lips curled and he pocketed the gun. With his left hand, he swept the sobbing mass of blubber to its feet and the fury of the night's upsets went into the swinging right that he threw personally for Hard-times Healy.

As Berlanger folded, the sirens shrieked and Culver's eyes widened. He didn't get it at first and when he did, he laughed unbelievingly.

"You were so sure you'd get this evidence out of the way that you even phoned for the cops," he said. "How damned obliging of you."

**THEY HAD** Berlanger whining his heart out in the station-house before Culver could get away to a private phone. When he did, he dialed a number wearily, got the city editor and leaned back against the booth. *"Blue Barrel,"* he said. "Kill that rubber-check item and the change-of-luck item for the final. Here's a new flash. Catch it!"

He had a pencil in his hand and he scribbled the words down as he dictated. "Not even the specialized knowledge of a rubber king is sufficient to beat the stretch for murder. The murderer of Hard-times Healy didn't stop to figure. When you steal the luck of a hard-times champion, that luck is sure to be bad."

He snapped the pencil in two as he left the booth. The dawn brigade would be battling the wheel at the Twin Moons and he was going back for a voluntary trick to relax. It would be nice for a few hours to sit around where nobody knew him and nobody gave a damn.

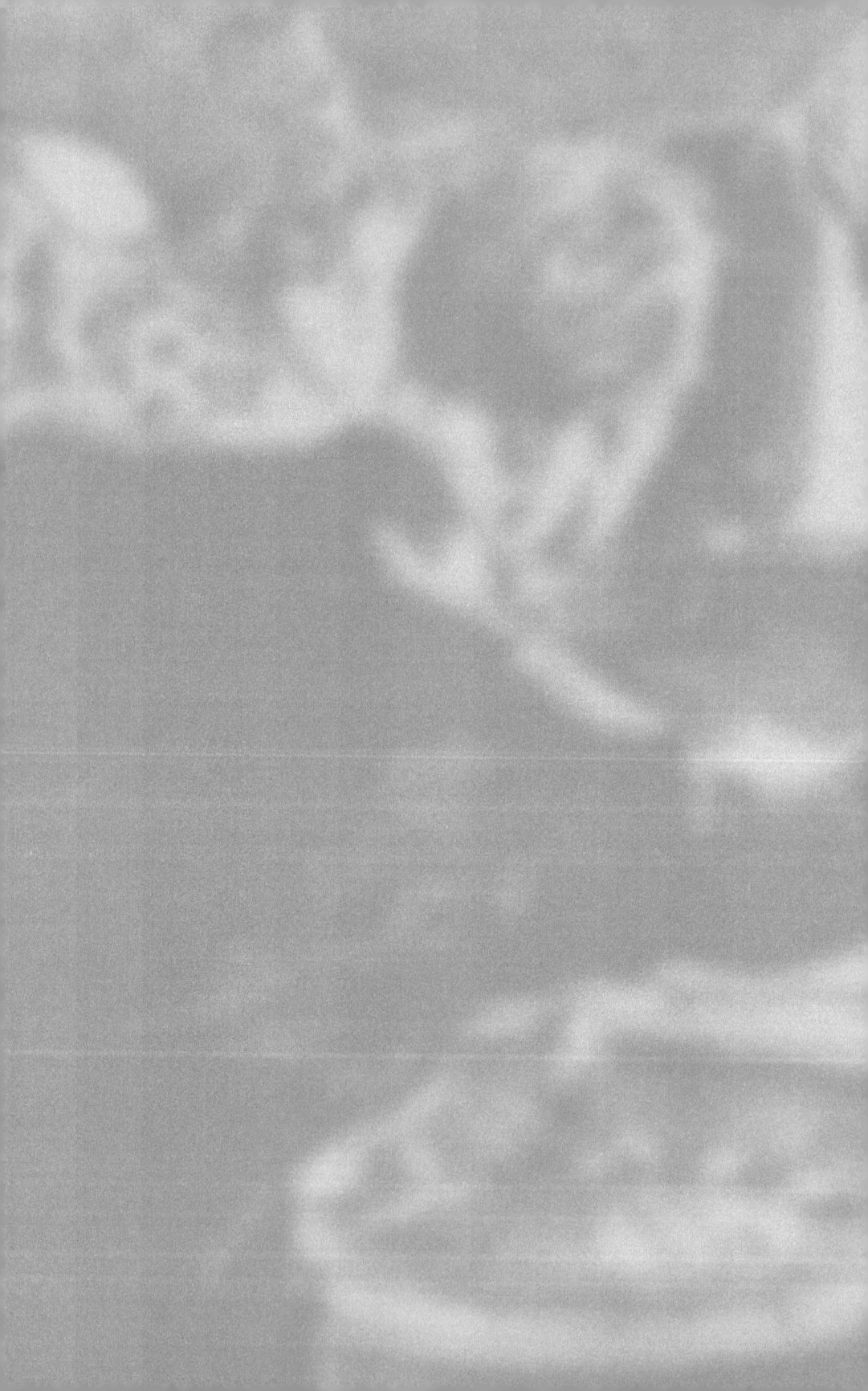

# DEATH ON THE DOUBLE-O

## WHICH JUST GOES TO PROVE THAT WHEN TWO MEN COMMIT ANOTHER MAN'S SUICIDE FOR HIM IT'S STILL MURDER.

**T**HE ROULETTE-WHEEL whirred and the little ball raced around to the music of it. Behind the wheel with the green eye-shade pulled low over his eyes, sat Dean Culver. He was the croupier, the dealer, the man who sat in one of the most conspicuous spots in town and who prided himself that in spite of that, he was practically unnoticed.

That is, he had so prided himself until tonight.

Nothing in Culver's expression betrayed the fact that tonight was different from any other. He moved like an automaton as he raked the chips in, distributed them, or whirled the little ball into its race. Hundreds of people saw him thus every evening at the Twin Moons, and there were regulars who played his wheel nightly. Scarcely one of them would have recognized him on the street. He was scenery, a sort of genie of the wheel, as mechanical as the wheel itself. He preferred it that way. But tonight—

The lantern-jawed man had been watching him steadily ever since copies of the *Star's* bull-dog edition had reached the Twin Moons. Sitting in one of the big easy chairs just clear of the field of play, he made no pretense of interest in any of the various games of chance. He was going through the motions of studying a racing form-sheet but his eyes measured Culver over the top of it, He had occupied the same spot last night but he had been watching Mark Creed then.

His name was Walter Lippen and he was a small-time highway contractor who had worked in, somehow, on a big deal. Though Culver did not know why he was in the Twin Moons, he suspected why he might be interested in Mark Creed. And he definitely didn't like to think of why the man might be interested in himself. Anybody's interest spelled danger for Dean Culver; particularly if that interest picked up on the arrival of the *Morning Star.*

**MARK CREED** hadn't even noticed the arrival of the newspaper—and he was the one who should have been interested. He was still engrossed in his task of placing dollars in thousand lots upon the wrong numbers of Culver's wheel. He had passed over many of those thousands and his eyes were sharp with panic, with the fear of losing so much, and of his inability to stop plunging. He was a bald-headed, pot-bellied little man with a red face and a gray-white neck. His hands trembled as he shoved in his chips, but he kept shoving them in.

"Hey, let's get a look at the *Barrel!* Maybe we'll be in it."

A dapper man was spreading the *Star* to bring Page Two to the top. He stood right behind Mark Creed and several others joined him at mention of the *Barrel.* The *Blue Barrel* with its automatic-pistol mast-head was the *Star's* exclusive feature; a slang column that had done for the world of crime what Winchell had done for Broadway. The chiselers and the double-crossers and the petty cheats feared it and when it leveled on a man, it rarely missed. It was read eagerly from the hamburger palaces to the exclusive clubs by people who liked to get a peek at tomorrow's crime headlines today, and who prided themselves that they could pick the story out of the anonymous *Blue Barrel's* cryptic hints.

The man who was spreading the paper passed right over the screaming front-page headlines—*SEEK GOVERNOR FOR STATE HIGHWAY GRAFT QUIZ*—and ran hastily through the first few items in the *Barrel.* Then, with the confidence of a column-addict who can spot the significant items, he read one aloud.

> "The biggest slice of satchel money ever paid in this state is slipping through the lily-whites of the wrong man. The blow-off will be terrific."

"Oh-oh." The man who read the item had been drinking and his voice had carry to it. "That means the governor didn't get the pay-off. Somebody glommed onto it." He struck a mock-dramatic pose and glanced sternly at his two companions. "Which of you guys has been shooting craps with the pee-pul's money?"

"Twenty-seven on the red."

Culver's hand was steady as he paid off two bets and raked in the rest of the chips. He was a smooth, efficient, well-oiled machine that nobody noticed except the lantern-jawed Walt Lippen who was still watching his every movement. Yet less than six feet away from Culver, the *Star's* crack column was being read and discussed. Across the table from him sat the man at which the deadliest slug of tonight's column was aimed.

And Dean Culver was the mysterious unknown, the hated, feared and sought-after *Blue Barrel.*

He seemed to be watching nobody, but Culver hadn't missed a shade of expression on the face of Mark Creed since the item was read. The man had jerked erect with the first sentence, then dropped his head like an ostrich that seeks to conceal its whole body by getting its eyes out of sight. His hands, trembling more violently than ever, pushed in triple the usual bet. The slate color that was natural enough on his neck was spreading over his entire face.

"Nine on the red."

Mark Creed foolishly had had a thousand dollars on *0-0* but he seemed scarcely aware of it as Culver scooped in the chips. He stared for a moment with eyes that were a trifle glazed and then his hand dropped the bulging lapel of his dinner jacket. It came up flashing.

Culver sensed what was coming even before the gleaming gun-barrel caught the light. The smooth, effortless rhythm of his work behind the wheel went into the fencer's thrust with which he sent the rake across the table.

Mark Creed had the gun-barrel in his mouth when the croupier's rake hooked into the trigger-guard.

Dean Culver flinched at the sharpness of the report. It slashed through the tense silence of the play at a dozen tables and boomed its echoes back from the four walls. Mark Creed swayed with his eyes staring whitely. A crystal tear from the big central chandelier fell to the floor and a woman screamed when it hit. Culver flipped the tiny gun from the end of the rake, caught it in his left hand, dropped it into his side pocket. His face was very white.

He was realizing suddenly that in saving the life of a would-be suicide, he had placed everyone else in the room in jeopardy. The slug that had torn a pendant from the chandelier might as well have torn life from a human heart.

"Play suspended."

He closed the wheel and walked around it. The man who had read the item from the *Blue Barrel* and one of his companions had grabbed the dazed Creed who did not quite realize yet that he was still alive. The floor-manager

He had the gun-barrel in his mouth when the croupier's
rake hooked into the trigger-guard.

and his assistant were crossing the room fast and Culver
left Mark Creed to them. He saw Larry Dane, his relief
man at the wheel, in the doorway and nodded to him.

"Take over for a while, Larry. I'm taking a walk."

Behind him, he was conscious that Walter Lippen had
risen from his easy chair. Another man rose from a similar
chair near the check-stand. Culver swore under his breath.

Somebody had something on him. The second man was
Lippen's partner in the highway business; a bull-necked,
heavy-chested lad named Bert Orker.

**IT TOOK** Culver less than three minutes to shake off
the clumsy shadowing of Bert Orker and he didn't have to
take a cab to do it. He was thinking rather grimly about
the hopeless, pot-bellied little fool who had tried to

commit suicide. It wasn't often that the *Blue Barrel* blasted at such inoffensive small game as that but the man had put himself on the spot.

Culver had known for a week that Mark Creed was the stooge into whose account the state-highway graft money had been paid and that the man was gambling with it. But Culver had created his *Blue Barrel* column to ferret out and destroy the human leeches who lived off the sweat of better men without taking risks; the framers and double-crossers and chiselers of the breed that had destroyed his own career, and those of many others as innocent as he had been when he served three years in an Illinois penitentiary.

Mere fools like Mark Creed didn't count, but when he had seen Lippen and Orker watching the man, he had known that the jig was up for Creed and that he might just as well beat the front page to the news.

Now Lippen and Orker were on him, too.

He made sure that he'd lost Orker and slipped into the lobby phone-booth of a quiet hotel. No one, not even the editors of the *Star,* knew the *Blue Barrel's* identity, but many anonymous tips came in to the paper addressed to the column. Some of them were good. There was one tonight.

The voice of Randall, the *Star's* city editor, came crisply over the wire. "Glad you called up, *B.B.* That tip of yours on the state-highway thing is kicking up dust. Lots of telephone since the rag hit the street. Mostly question-askers. One of them claims he has a tip on more dirt. Call Northern Nine-seven-nine-eight. Ask for Mr. Graystone."

"O.K. Thanks, Randall. I'll let you know if it's level."

Culver hung up and sat staring for a moment at the phone. Northern 9798 was the number of the Twin Moons—but he didn't know any Mr. Graystone.

"Fancy that now," he said quietly. "We'll have a look."

He dialed the number, disguised his voice for the benefit of the girl at the Twin Moons' board and waited while his man was called. He didn't recognize the husky voice that identified itself as "Graystone." He hadn't expected to.

"This is the *Blue Barrel,*" Culver said. "Talk fast if you've got anything. I've got a one-minute limit on calls."

He wasn't kidding about that, either. People had planted stooges on the phone with him before while they traced the call and tried to race him to the hang-up. He expected them to do that and none of them had even come close. Graystone seemed disconcerted.

"All right," he said hesitantly, "but this is serious. I've got dope on the state-highway racket."

"Spill it."

"It's this, see. An item you can run like this. 'What behind-the-scenes figure in the state-highway investigation has abandoned his hot-spot haunts to join the governor in seclusion?'"

Culver raised his eye-brows. Somebody has spent time and thought on that item. They had it in pretty much the tone he used in the column. But he growled into the mouthpiece: "I'll bite, guy. What figure has?"

"Isn't that enough. You don't run any more than that."

"I know more when I don't. Spcak up or hang up."

"All right. You're a hard guy. Well, the lad that's pulling out is the guy you ran the item about, Mark Creed. He bought his tickets this afternoon. That gambling-loss stuff was a stall you fell for. He's taking the dough to the governor.... If you don't believe me, wait till it's news."

There was a click at the other end of the line. Culver got up and moved swiftly out of the booth. He was a block away and around two corners before he stopped to light a cigarette. "The lug gave me a tip at that," he said grimly.

**HE WASN'T** thinking about the stuff that the man had told him but it was interesting to discover that somebody had a reason for planting such an idea. Mark Creed wasn't joining the governor and hadn't planned on joining them. Culver was willing to bet heavily on that. He didn't believe that Creed knew any more about where the governor had gone than anyone else did. The state executive was merely lying low till he saw how the cat jumped on the investigation that the rival party had stirred up. He didn't need people like Mark Creed for company and the last thing he'd want at the moment was the money that would tie him up to the bribe charges.

But somebody was going to a lot of trouble planting a disappearance for Mark Creed.

The regular newsboy was selling his papers on the corner and Culver nipped him a half-dollar. "Son," he said, "do you think you could call Northern Nine-seven-nine-eight in five minutes and ask for Mr. Graystone."

The youngster pocketed the coin with a deft movement. "Sure. What do I do when he answers?"

Culver shrugged. "Just hang up."

He went on to the Twin Moons and killed a moment with the girl who handled telephone calls. Bert Orker had not come back and Culver imagined that the man was still trying to pick up a lost trail. The phone rang while Culver was checking his hat and coat with the girl at the checkstand.

"Mr. Graystone!"

The telephone-girl's voice was raised as she sent the page-boy off. Culver lighted a cigarette. In about twenty seconds, the page-boy was back with the lantern-jawed Walt Lippen in tow. Lippen was one of those men who manage to look slovenly and not quite clean even in evening clothes. There was a yellow stain in one corner of his mouth like the drool-stain of a tobacco-chewer. Culver heard him say "Graystone!" into the phone. He looked a little puzzled and a little expectant when he said it. Then he looked mad. He turned savagely on the telephone girl.

"They hung up," he growled.

She smiled back at him. "I'm sorry, Mr. Graystone."

"Well, don't call me again unless you have somebody on the line."

**HE SWUNG** his shoulders and went muttering back to the big room; a lean, powerful, rangy man who walked with his head held forward. Culver watched him thoughtfully. For a man who had come up off a truck, Walt Lippen was carrying a lot of nerves tonight. If he had been as smart as he was tough, he'd have figured that second call as a stall and looked around for someone watching him who might be the *Blue Barrel*. It was on little business like that that the tough monkeys lost out.

"Hanlon's office, Mr. Culver, before you go back on the trick." The page-boy was at his elbow and Culver nodded.

"Right."

Dollar Hanlon was the front office and biggest shareholder of the Twin Moons, Culver's boss and a square shooter. He didn't know that Culver was the *Blue Barrel* but he suspected his past and he didn't ask questions when the answers didn't make much difference to him.

Tonight Dollar Hanlon was indulging a mild blow-up of his own. He had the *Morning Star* in his hand and Mark Creed seated in the most comfortable chair in his office.

Creed was still a sickly shade of white and there were marks of tears on his face. He was a very sick, paunchy, half-hysterical man and he was no longer young. Dollar Hanlon was no longer young himself, but he was built as solidly as a battleship and he wore his gray hair as he would have worn any other scars that he acquired in the battle with life. He slapped the *Blue Barrel* column with the back of his hand.

"Have you seen this yet, Culver?"

Actually Culver hadn't; he'd merely written it via phone dictation. He shook his head. "I heard some of it read downstairs just before our friend here tried to dutch it."

*"Umph!* That's it. You heard this crack?"

He pointed with one thick forefinger to the leaded-type paragraph that the bystander had read aloud downstairs.

Culver nodded. "So what?"

"So Mr. Creed here is the wrong man that's been spending the dough. This graft dough was paid into his account and he was being paid to play dummy and keep it warm. He's been shooting it across our tables. Culver, I ask you. How in hell could we know?"

"We couldn't." Culver's voice was crisp.

Hanlon banged the desk-top with the paper.

"The public won't stop to figure, Culver. Nobody loses big cash in this place without being checked up. A bank clerk couldn't lose the bank's sugar here. I wouldn't let him. Mr. Creed here was losing money out of his own account. I checked that up, damn it!"

HANLON WAS walking up and down. Huddled miserably in his chair, Mark Creed watched him. Mark Creed had probably been a pretty good man once but something had died in him when he pulled the trigger tonight, even if his body lived on.

"Let me go," he said. "I won't do you any harm. I'll get away from here—"

Dollar Hanlon spread his hands. "You hear the guy, Culver? He's still going to slaughter himself. And just get a mental picture of what the wash-up will do to us. We're the motive."

"Sure." Culver was looking narrowly at Mark Creed.

Dollar Hanlon misinterpreted the look. "It isn't a stall to poker us into dishing the seventy grand back, Culver. Mr. Creed ain't that kind of a customer. It's level but it's still lousy."

Mark Creed inhaled with a noisy, sucking sound and came to his feet. There was a wild look in his eyes. "A man's life is his own business if anything is," he said. "I don't want any money back. I want the liberty that any citizen is entitled to. I want to get out of here—get far away from here and—"

Dollar Hanlon spread his hands again and looked helplessly at Culver, then grimly at Creed. "It ain't that I care whether you dutch it or not. That's your business, Mr. Creed. Sure it is. But we can't let you do it. It's going to come out that you lost heavy sugar here if you dutch. I just naturally ain't going to see my place spread over page-one newsprint with this dirty highway mess. Not any. By the time that some papers got through, I'd practically be the guy that took the graft; complete with cartoons. Nix!"

Creed's lips were trembling but he was still on his feet and waving his hands. There was a glazed film over his eyes and he was beyond the power of argument. "You can't hold me," he shouted. "You can't keep me from doing what I want to do. I won't live! I won't face it all. I've thrown away my reputation. I've betrayed a trust...."

He made a dive for the desk and a swooping grab for Dollar's paper knife. Hanlon beat him to the grab and knocked the knife to the floor with his right hand. With his left, he shoved Creed back on his heels.

"Take him away, Culver," he said. "He's your job. Get him home and sit with him till he comes out of it. Order in a couple of bright blondes or a case of liquor. Anything reasonable. Only kind of keep him alive till he snaps out of it."

Mark Creed was swaying on his feet, staring hopelessly at Hanlon. Like a man with too much liquor, he was numb to all but a single idea. He was emotionally jagged. He groped behind him suddenly for the chair and sat down.

Culver looked at him thoughtfully. "We'll get along," he said.

He was not thinking so much about the problem of keeping the man from being snatched. There had been a quarter of a million in the highway-graft satchel and the seventy grand that Creed had lost was not a very big hole in a chunk like that. That phony tip to the *Blue Barrel* had been paving the way for a disappearance that Mark Creed had not planned voluntarily. Somebody was laying the groundwork for snatching this poor little sap and bleeding him for the rest of that dough. When Walt Lippen fell for the fake phone call to "Graystone," he'd tipped off the identity of the potential snatchers; but Culver, as Culver, couldn't use information that he possessed only as the *Blue Barrel*. To do so would be to risk exposure. He extended his hand to Mark Creed.

"Mr. Creed," he said, "we're going to have a talk."

**LIPPEN AND** Orker were slow on the draw. Dean Culver had his man out of the Twin Moons and into a cab before either of them knew that he had left Hanlon's office. Mark Creed was suddenly like so much putty. He was passing through the limp, indifferent stage that follows an emotional debauch. He sat in the cab with his head pulled into the collar of his topcoat and his chin on his chest. Culver was satisfied to have him like that. He addressed himself to the driver.

"Just cruise around for a while."

He was trying to find thinking-time. Lippen and Orker were not to be underestimated. They'd been hurried by circumstances tonight and they'd fumbled a bit, but they were hard men. They had to be tough to batter their way up from the hard-boiled ranks that had graduated them. And they would know where Creed lived.

"I'll have enough to do with this crackpot on my hands...."

Culver looked sidewise at Mark Creed. The idea of Creed's place as a spot to spend the night did not sound attractive. There'd be less chance of interference from Lippen and Orker in Culver's own quarters or in a neutral spot like a quiet hotel. But either of those spots would be pretty tough if Creed escaped the Culver vigilance and succeeded in killing himself. Suicides were often pretty resourceful and it could happen. If it did, the police might not accept the fact that it was suicide and Culver would be in a poisonous spot. Hanlon, of course, would back him up; but Dollar Hanlon was hardly a grade-A, certified police witness and a jury wouldn't like his profession.

Culver sighed. "The Burlington Arms!" he said.

He was going to have to chance Creed's apartment; even if he had to stand siege as well as stand watch.

It was a small apartment and one in which the regularly provided hotel service made servants unnecessary. It was on the twelfth floor and there was an entry-hall, a large living-room with only partially filled built-in bookcases, a small bedroom, a breakfast-nook and a green-and-white kitchen. The only luxury touch was provided by the balcony-porch that ran past the two living-room windows and provided width enough for several porch chairs and two potted palms.

Culver didn't like the porch. It provided too neat a diving platform for a man who wanted to end it all. He didn't like the fact, either, that the adjoining balconies were close enough for an agile man to change porches with a minimum of risk. The set-up made it look like a busy night.

"I'm a ruined man. Why don't you leave me?"

Mark Creed had thrown himself down in one of the living-room chairs. His voice was almost a wail.

Culver halted in the middle of the room. "Why spread destruction? You'd just about ruin the Twin Moons if you dutched out. I work for it."

"I've ruined everything else." Creed locked his fingers together, his arms between his knees. "I had a very successful bank once, Mr. Culver. I contributed a lot of money to campaign funds for Governor Porter's party. The depression ruined my bank...."

His voice caught, "I was pretty desperate but I still had my reputation. I had to offer that for sale when I had nothing else left to sell. They bought it, Governor Porter's party. You seem to know the story. It wasn't strange for me to have large sums in the bank. I'd dealt in finance all my life. The governor didn't want any large sums in his account until he saw how matters stood. He—they—used mine. I got a salary. I wasn't supposed to touch the principal."

He choked up and waved his hands. "I did. I had a good salary, but I betrayed the men who gave it to me. I had a gambling streak. Most bankers have and won't admit it I couldn't trade in securities. I wasn't used to games. I—"

He left the chair so fast that Culver was taken by surprise. Off-balance, Culver dived for him and stopped a vicious straight left that rocked him. Creed was past him like a shot and headed straight through the bedroom for the bathroom beyond. Culver cursed and pushed himself up from the floor. He hit the bathroom door with his shoulder just as Creed closed it, and landed on the man as he fastened his fingers on the case of an old-fashioned razor.

**THE GLAZE** was back on Creed's eyes and he had the strength of a maniac. Culver slapped the razor out of his hand but the little pot-bellied banker found two punches in his system that shook Culver to the base of his spine. Then they were locked in a fierce embrace on the floor and Mark Creed was an awkward package to hold. He twisted his body out of a series of grips and got his fingers on the razor-case once more. Culver's fingers slipped down his arm and fastened hard upon his wrist.

There was a thumping sound in the living-room that Culver heard without having time to register. Fighting the hold on his wrist, Creed was shaking the ugly straight blade from the case. His eyes held a mad glitter and there was drool running from the corner of his mouth. His right hand was free and he hit Culver again and again with it as Culver concentrated on holding the razor-hand down. A foot hit the bedroom floor, then a startled voice broke above the struggling men.

"Hey there! What's this all about?"

Creed seemed unconscious of the interruption and Culver took a chance. He had a flash of Bert Orker's broad face and he gambled that Mark Creed would not be given a chance to use the razor. He released his grip on the man's wrist suddenly and smashed his right fist home to the flabby jaw. If he had missed, he would have had the razor to contend with—but he didn't miss.

He came up twisting as he felt Creed's body go limp and Walter Lippen stepped past the poised Orker. Culver saw the gun in his hand and he caught the flash of its arc; but he was in no position to avoid it. The gun-barrel caught him on the side of the head as he turned with the blow and he felt himself pitching forward.

Lippen's voice had a snarl in it. "You can always talk to these tough guys better," he said, "after you've softened them up."

He stepped across Culver's body and bent above Mark Creed. The little ex-banker seemed to have forgotten the razor and the strength that was in him a few minutes earlier was spent. He was moaning softly and saying something in a mumbling undertone that did not quite make sense. Culver's head was spinning and his stomach was threatening to revolt on him from sock-shock, but he did not lose his consciousness nor his sense of what was going on. He merely lay where he had fallen and took advantage of his old role of being unnoticed.

Lippen was shaking the dazed Mark Creed savagely. "Come out of it!" he said hoarsely. "You're going to take a little trip."

Creed shook himself in revolt against the manhandling. "I won't," he said. "I won't go with anybody."

"Maybe you better tap him, too. We'll take him out like he was drunk." Bert Orker's voice had a rasp to it.

"No, we won't! This cookie isn't the type that goes out drunk. He's going out of this apartment with a packed bag an he's going down the elevator without either one of us showing. And he ain't talking a word to elevator men neither. He's going to get the idea if we have to sit with him all night."

Walter Lippen had savage command in his voice. He had evidently rehearsed all of the eventualities in this play, and he was hard enough to ram through on a single track once he had laid his plan. Bert Orker was just as hard, perhaps, but he had the kind of mind that is easily confused—and this job evidently had him scared. He wanted to slam into it the quickest way and get it over.

"What about the guy you conked?" he said.

"He fits in. This bird, Creed, will be glad to bail out when...." Lippen let the sentence dangle in the air while he resumed his shaking of the mumbling banker. Culver felt, grimly, that he could finish that sentence. He had made his deductions about Lippen when he found out that the contractor was the man who had tried to peddle him the phony tip on Mark Creed's leaving town.

Lippen had known, when he talked to Culver on the phone, that Creed had just attempted suicide and that the man was not going to jump town. Lippen had been watching Creed spend money before the *Blue Barrel* cracked the tip. And Lippen's attempt to palm off that story about Creed jumping out to join the governor on the most widely read—and believed—column in town explained the shift of attention to Culver.

**LIPPEN HAD** figured that the *Blue Barrel* item would scare Creed—as it did scare him—and he figured that Creed would ask for protection on his trip home. Culver was usually the man assigned to protection jobs. It all added up neatly.

"Creed! You listen to me. You've got one chance of getting out of the mess you're in. But you've got to play ball with us. We won't play rough unless you make us."

The lanky, lantern-jawed Lippen was a shadow outlined monstrously on the floor. Culver could watch his movements in silhouette without raising his head. He was shaking Creed again to emphasize his words. Culver moved one hand under his body, balanced on it and came up suddenly with a twist that put him sitting with his back to the wall. His right hand moved in and out of his armpit as he rolled, and his gun was level when his back touched the wall.

"Hold it, everybody!" he said grimly. "Listen to me, Creed, if you want to do any listening."

Culver's hand felt light but he could see the three men pretty clearly through the slight haze before his eyes. Orker had his gun in his hand but he had let it drop halfway to his knee and he had had sense enough not to raise it in the face of the draw. Culver gave him a curt nod.

"Drop it!"

Orker's fingers went lax and the gun hit the floor. Lippen had put his own gun away but the expression on his gaunt, heavy-lipped face was primarily that of disgust for Orker. Culver had an idea that Lippen wouldn't have dropped a gun that he had in his hand. Mark Creed was shaking his head stupidly. The banker had died once tonight within his own imagination and his experiences since then had been a series of mental and physical shocks through which he had moved half-insane.

Yet upon such a weak reed must Culver lean. He was not in a position to do anything about Walt Lippen and Bert

Orker and they, eventually, would figure that out for themselves. The law was out of the question. It would not only put the Twin Moons on the front pages in a big way, but it would put Culver there where he couldn't afford to be. It would be pretty nearly as bad as if Mark Creed were snatched. Any search for him would bring a noisy backtrail to the Twin Moons with the resultant squawk that gambling-houses bred graft and dishonesty.

Culver drew further upon the deductions that he had made from the phony tip and hurled those deductions at the dazed banker. "Creed," he said, "these two muggs had a contracting business that was just big enough to get onto the fringe of those state-highway contracts, but they were the first to unload when the investigation started. They've been supplying the governor's enemies with their dope on the contracts for a promise that they'll be let out in the clear."

"Why, you—"

Walt Lippen's eyes were lidded almost shut and there was a snarling twist to his long lips. Culver moved the gun as the man stepped forward.

"One more step, Lippen!"

There was ice in his voice. He was coming slowly to his feet, sliding his shoulder blades up along the wall. He had the gun steady. Orker was in a crouch and his eyes swerved regretfully to the gun on the floor. Mark Creed was passing his hand across his forehead dazedly as though he were striving to comprehend what Culver had been telling him and finding the effort a strain. Culver lashed at him relentlessly. He had only one plan and it depended upon Mark Creed.

"They want to kidnap you, Creed," he said. "They know you've got the governor's account. They'd bleed it out of you, make you sign checks to them. They want to double-cross every other contractor that plays with highways and ruin them in the legislature, and they want to grab the graft that they are so virtuous about, to make their own business big. They're filthy rats, Creed, and—"

A righteously indignant Creed who got that picture could seize this moment, call in the police, confess his own shame and denounce the two men who had pulled down a dozen careers with their greed. It would still be disgrace for Creed but he'd be a hero in disgrace.

But the man was too far gone.

Culver had been concentrating on him and watching Lippen too closely. His guard had been a bit too relaxed as far as Orker was concerned, and he realized it too late. Bert Orker dived in with the word "rats."

**CULVER FIRED** and the shot snapped over the diving man's head. Orker was close-coupled and under-slung and he packed his weight between his shoulders and his chest. Culver felt a ramming impact that was like the slap of a locomotive's front end. He went catapulting back against the wall and as Orker followed his dive with a slugging fist, Culver clubbed twice with the gun-muzzle. He went to the floor with Orker, and Orker rolled desperately away from him to escape the gun-barrel. As he did, he kicked out with his right foot.

Culver felt a numbing sensation that ran along his entire arm as the kick landed on the point of his elbow. The gun leaped from his fingers and Orker scrambled for it.

"Look out, you! Drop it—"

Walt Lippen's voice was so sharp with command that even Orker and Culver hesitated. Mark Creed had come out of his lethargy once more with that same uncanny speed of the obsessed that he had demonstrated twice before. One leap gave him the gun that Orker had dropped earlier at Culver's command, and he came up with it just as Lippen was leaping to his partner's assistance. There was only one thought in Lippen's mind as that gun came up—but there was an entirely different thought in Creed's.

Lippen didn't know.

He was directly in the muzzle of that gun for a split second and he didn't gamble on the next fraction. He fired from the hip.

**MARK CREED** vented one strangling cry, pivoted on his toes and pressed the trigger as he spun. Bert Orker took the bullet squarely between the eyes.

Culver saw him die and he had the gun that had lain between them in the moment that Orker's soul blinked out. His fingers closed on it but he knew that he would not have time to fire it if Lippen followed through on his turn and pumped another shot his way. With the same swooping motion that gave him the gun, he plunged on into Lippen's legs and took the man to the floor.

Lippen cursed obscenely and missed the one thrust that he had time to make. Culver hit him squarely on the temple with the gun-barrel and wiggled away from him as he went limp.

"'That makes us square—and plus," he whispered.

He was sick and dizzy and aching but it was no time to let down. The shots had tenants of the apartment house up and out in the hall in a trice. Someone was banging on the door. It would be only a very few minutes before a cop would be kicking that door down. Culver looked down at the shambles in the room.

Mark Creed was quite dead and his face, for the first time in a wild night, was peaceful and relaxed. Walt Lippen lay on his back with the gun that had shot Creed still clutched in his fist.

There was a poetic justice in that which satisfied something in Culver's soul. When the cops rolled in on that scene, Lippen could tell any story that he liked but he'd never argue past that gun. He was signed, sealed and delivered and Culver could see no scandal for the Twin Moons in a murder that occurred in a man's own apartment. He moved swiftly toward the living-room. He remembered that the balcony abutted on the balcony of the next apartment and it was easy to figure his play.

The two men would not have slipped in so easily if they had not been smart enough to grab that next-door apartment when they planned their act. Culver could go back the way they had come and mingle out in the hall with the aroused tenants. He took a last look at Lippen.

"Fancy you making an appeal to this governor," he said, "when you face the chair. Fancy it. And he has two years yet to run."

He was framing the wording of an item for his column as he scaled the balcony, and he completed it when he was drifting out through the packed mass of tenants that the cops were shooing off the floor.

> The inside on the latest slaughter sensation is that the timing was bad. A jury will still insist that when two men commit another man's suicide for him, the name is murder....

He phoned it in and headed for the Twin Moons. It would be easy to fix an air-tight alibi there that would stand against any story that Lippen might tell. He might even

slip back into his place behind the wheel and a dozen repu-
table people would swear that he had been there all evening.

After all, nobody ever noticed the croupier. It was one
of the delightful features of the job.

# A MAN'S LAST HOURS

THE VENGEANCE-KILLING,
SCHEDULED TO TAKE PLACE
THAT NIGHT BY THE LIGHT OF
THE TWIN MOONS, HERALDED
TROUBLE WITH A CAPITAL T FOR
THE PROPRIETOR OF THAT SWANK
HOUSE-OF-CHANCE. YET THE
POLICE, UNABLE TO ACT BEFORE
THE MURDER-HOUR, WERE HOG-
TIED. AND ONLY DEAN CULVER,
WHOSE JOB WAS BETTING ON THE
FUTURE, COULD DISCOVER THE
ONE DESPERATE WAY OUT.

**T**HE CROWD was three deep around the roulette-table despite the fact that it was early evening when the Twin Moons dining-room could usually be depended upon to outdraw the betting-salon. Some plunger from out of town was running a big streak, and crowds usually follow sensations.

Behind the spinning wheel, Dean Culver sat with his eye-shade pulled low. He was the croupier, the man whom nobody noticed. Night after night, he sat in the most conspicuous spot in one of the town's most popular places and attracted no more attention than the furniture. He called the play, tossed the ball to the spinning mechanism, and plied his rake as the numbers came up and the chips went out or came in.

"Seventeen in the black."

He was paying off the plunger again. A light hand touched his shoulder. "Hanlon's office, Culver. I'll take over."

Larry Dane, the change-off man on the wheel, was standing just behind him. Culver nodded his head. "O.K.," he said.

It was done like that, a simple exchange between plays. The crowd never noticed the difference. One man or another, the wheel went around and around. Culver walked quietly across the room. He wore the regulation dinner-jacket, and there was nothing to mark him apart from other men or to make him remembered. He preferred it like that. If once he attracted too much attention, he was through.

There were men playing at his wheel who would kill him within twenty-four hours if they knew his real identity.

He passed out into the big reception-hall. It was quiet, dignified, furnished in taste, more like a parlor in a big hotel than like the rendezvous room of a gambling-house. To the right of the door to the street there was a large dining-room that was more than a mere front for the other activities of the Twin Moons. People dined at the Twin Moons who never gambled there. Culver swung left to the heavily carpeted stairs that led to the upper floor and the private office of Dollar Hanlon.

Hanlon was seated behind his mahogany desk, a big man with iron-gray hair, clear eyes and a firm chin. To Hanlon's left sat a red-faced man in a gray suit, Sergeant Driscoll of the homicide squad. Culver nodded his greet-ings and raised one eyebrow in the direction of Driscoll.

"Somebody been getting slaughtered around here?" he asked.

Hanlon grunted explosively. "Naw. But do you know what that fool, Doherty, did?"

"Let someone in with a soup spot on his vest?" Culver made himself at ease. Hanlon was the boss, but Hanlon could be kidded. Doherty was the downstairs-man and greeter, and Hanlon kept him on the job while he forever grumbled about him. Hanlon didn't rise to humor this evening.

"Monk Menger got out of the pen today," he said. "Tonight, Doherty lets Sid Weyler into my place. Does that mean anything to you?"

"I'm away ahead of you." Culver's face was suddenly grim, the lines bracketed deep around his mouth.

**THEY HAD** taken Monk Menger out of a courtroom nine years ago with the word "frame" on his lips and a publicly registered oath that he'd kill Sid Weyler the day he came out. It was one of those things, but Monk Menger was out and the underworld would be sitting back and waiting. Monk Menger and Sid Weyler had been partners in the dope-racket, and Menger had been a pretty big shot. He'd be a small-time punk if he didn't do anything about Sid Weyler now—and he'd had nine years to think about it. Dollar Hanlon was worrying a cigar.

"Weyler, the big heel, is stowing a feed downstairs now," he growled. "He'll take his time and then he'll play the wheel. Sure. He'll be right out in a public place where nobody can criticize him, and it's Menger's play."

"Doherty doesn't have to let Menger in, too."

"Naw. He'd be sap enough to do it, though. It's when Weyler has to leave that we get burned. We always give big customers protection home with their dough when they ask for it. He's figuring on that."

Culver hadn't changed expression, but there had been no joke about his statement that he was away ahead of Dollar Hanlon on the first sum-up. He was the one who was usually picked to escort the heavy winners home. It would be very nice for Sid Weyler, if Sid could euchre Dean Culver into shooting Monk Menger for him. That way, Monk would die in a suck-up and there'd be no flare-back on Weyler, no cop theories on feuds, that would stand before a jury. Culver shrugged and looked toward Sergeant Driscoll.

"There're still a few cops working for the city, aren't there?" he said.

"That's what I thought," Dollar Hanlon was glaring at the plainclothesman. A faint smile crossed Driscoll's grim lips. "We don't pinch anybody for crimes that haven't happened yet," he said. "It just ain't legal."

He tapped the ash from his cigar against his heel, That was the cop position and they were sitting pat on it, Sid Weyler had been a pain to the cops for years, a slick-labor racketeer who beat every rap that they tried to hang on him. Monk Menger, of course, was just somebody who was better off in the can. To have Weyler removed by Menger, under circumstances that made Menger's conviction a cinch, would be just too perfect from a cop angle.

Dollar Hanlon looked with irate helplessness at Culver. "We're it," he said. "For the first time since we've been open, we send a customer out to be killed. If we don't, we have to take on a job of killing to do, with a lot of lousy publicity on the side."

Driscoll was pulling on his cigar. "Culver could forget to load his gun," he said.

Hanlon pushed a box of cigars across the desk. "You're a big help," he agreed. "Here, make yourself sick. I'm talking to Culver...."

He led Culver out into the hall. There was a moment of silence after they reached the little private conference-room that Hanlon reserved for moments like this. Hanlon was shaking his head.

"Culver," he said, "Monk Menger's going to do it. I called a newspaper guy I know. They're keeping tabs on him. He's over at Zorro's and he's boasting that he's going to chill

Weyler. He's got to come through even if he's got no more privacy than if he rodded somebody during a police line-up."

Culver smoked quietly. "So what?"

"So, the only play is for you to go over to Zorro's and cover Monk Menger. I'll send somebody else home with Sid Weyler, if I have to."

Culver's lips twisted wryly. "You mustn't have anything in mind for the future that I figure in very much."

Hanlon matched him with a hard grin. "I wouldn't send you anyplace unless I figured that you'd come back, somehow."

Culver turned to the door. "That 'somehow' is the catch to it. But I'll try Zorro's," he said.

**IT TOOK** less than ten minutes for Culver to change into a suit of dark blue that had been worn often enough to be inconspicuous anywhere. It took him five more minutes to reach Big John Zorro's.

In all the city, there was no place like Big John's. You could order an Italian dinner there, and get a good one, or you could order hot money at discount prices, an honest gunman out of work or a neat piece of forgery. You'd be equally well served in all cases, and Big John would be as innocent as a baby of the whole transaction. Through the whole deal, he'd be just a big good-natured Italian who liked to "introduce my frands togedder." When he got his cut, he'd be as grateful as a child for his "gift."

Culver stopped outside for a moment below the glittering neon sign of red and blue, then shrugged and plugged down the three steps to the basement-entrance. Big John was standing inside the door, as usual. He beamed when he saw Culver.

Culver went for him, lunging, as the gun cracked three times.

"Ah, good evening, Jones, my frand."

"Evening, John."

Culver allowed his hand to be pumped and hid his grin. It was one of Big John's little pretenses that he knew everyone who came into his place and he called everyone "Jones, my frand." It was a good gag. If a man corrected him, he apologized—and had the right name thereafter. Occasionally, he would actually hit a Jones and that was perfect. Culver let the Jones stand.

About him the lights were dim, and his table was in a corner. There was a small dance-floor surrounded by the favored tables of good spenders. Monk Menger had one of these.

He did not look like a man just out of stir. He was wearing dinner-clothes and had a couple of girls of the chorusgirl type with him, one on either side. The others of his party were small-time chiselers who dated back to the days when Menger was a big shot. The tough boys, who counted, weren't present. They were waiting to see how Monk Menger made out before they joined any of his parties.

And Menger was boasting. He was pretty well lit, bragging about what he was going to do to Sid Weyler. Culver could read his lips. The man had ample lips to read. He was short, squat and ape-like with a big mouth and sloping jaw. He was throwing a party and before midnight, he was going to blaze down Sid Weyler.

"It will be a good act if it happens." Culver placed his order, then made his way to a phone booth. Every eye in the place seemed fixed upon Monk Menger's table. Culver passed, unnoticed. That, too, was a laugh.

If the people who patronized Zorro's knew Culver, for who and for what he was, he'd attract more attention than a dozen Monk Mengers—and he wouldn't figure to live as long. He slipped into a phone booth and called the *Morning Star.*

"Randall? This is the *Blue Barrel.* Catch an item fast, for tonight's bull-dog. Here it is. The inside on why a well-known labor racketeer will not be killed tonight by a well-known ex-convict is that preservation is the first law of nature, and that a man can be awfully sore and still not be sore enough to pull a trigger in a goldfish-bowl."

"Hey—you're putting yourself on a limb." Randall's voice was startled. "Menger's got to—"

"I know. Take bets on it."

Culver hung up and slid back to his table. That item would go into type fast and it would appear in a first-page box with a cut of an automatic pistol at its head. People would read it and discuss it and believe it. The *Blue Barrel* was a local institution. What Winchell had done with a gossip-column, the *Blue Barrel* had done with a crime-column—got out in front ahead of the headlines. There was one difference. Men had gone to jail, and men had died, because the *Blue Barrel* leveled at them. Like the weapon from which it got its name, the column fired slugs—slugs of type.

And Dean Culver, who spent most of his life as the unnoticed man in the green eye-shade, was the anonymous *Blue Barrel.*

**HE ATE** slowly, watched Monk Menger—and then he saw the frail youth at the table beyond his own. The man appeared to be in the last stages of tuberculosis, and his big, dark eyes fixed on Menger's table with a sort of desperate fascination. His lower lip was trembling, and Culver had the impression of chattering teeth behind the man's lips. The man's thin hand fumbled under the napkin on the table-top.

That was the tip-off. Culver was out of his chair as the gun cleared the napkin. The frail youth came to his feet, and the gun swung through a shining arc to level full on Monk Monger. Monk fixed startled eyes on Death's glittering symbol—and Culver suddenly dived.

The youth with the gun had a moment of indecision, warring impulses, desperate resolve. In that moment, Culver hit him. Culver's lips were pressed tight, his eyes were fixed on the gun. His left hand flashed clear, and he had the youth's wrist in his grip. It was like bending a toothpick back. The gun fell to the floor, and the weapon-wielder went as limp as a straw man. Culver swept him off his feet and slammed him back again into the chair that he had vacated.

The surrounding tables were in turmoil. Waiters were closing in, and Monk Menger's party was standing. Monk had his hand buried in his armpit, a belated gesture that did him no good—and that would have done him no good even if he had made it sooner. Culver shook the man he had grabbed.

"Keep your mouth shut, mugg," he said.

**HE WAVED** the waiters back, a hard crew of huskies who could—and did—do many things besides wait on the customers of Big John. Big John, himself, was coming down the aisle like a human locomotive. Culver beckoned to him.

"Get us out, John, and quiet," he said. Zorro's eyes bit into him. As a casual customer, a man might be "Jones, my frand," but when that customer asked for anything, John had to know which Jones was doing the asking.

"This fellow should be pinch," he said.

"Sure. But I'm paid to follow him around and keep him out of trouble. I did."

Culver nodded toward the trembling youth and tapped his forehead significantly. He had already started to propel him toward an exit. They were up against a wall with a phalanx of waiters between them and the diners at the tables. Big John was mad. Every available man of his, that wasn't on this particular party, was busy around the dining-room, attempting to restore order. Things had moved so fast that very few people had seen what happened, and rumors were flying. Somebody said that Sid Weyler had come in, and people were straining to see.

"I do not know this feller. I do not know you."

"O.K. You don't want a pinch in your place tonight, John."

"Me, I never want the pinch in my place. What the hell?"

"O.K. I'm taking the kid out, see? He didn't do a thing. Monk Menger isn't going into court to swear that the kid pointed a gun at him, I hope? You see how it is?"

Big John saw. It was a dirty situation from his point of view and, under ordinary circumstances, he'd have had a half-dozen huskies take Culver and the youth out in the alley. They'd be worked over plenty, and Big John would swear that he'd never seen either of them. Tonight, he didn't want anything to detract from the drama of Monk Menger's return. It was bringing Big John business, and there would be curious hundreds coming into the place for weeks if Monk Menger shot Sid Weyler tonight and the word got out that he had primed himself at Zorro's for the killing. There would even be saps who would pay an extra cover-charge to sit at the table that Monk Menger had occupied.

"All right," he said. "You take him out quick. Never again come into this place."

Culver didn't hear the rest. He was hustling the kid along, and the kid was a limp parcel. They reached the sidewalk by a side exit, with a few assorted Italian oaths curling around their ears. Culver steered a course down the block.

"Mugg," he said, "you've got a lot to tell me."

**THEY STOPPED** at a white-lightning joint where there were booths, and where the customers who weren't too drunk to listen in on conversation were too indifferent to listen in. Culver studied his prisoner across the table-top, with grim eyes.

The fellow was no more than twenty-five but the white plague was strongly in the saddle. He was coughing hard when he came into the place, and had another fit of it when he took the drink that he needed. He had probably been a good-looking young man once. He was a walking skeleton now.

"What's your name?" Culver shot the question at him fast.

"Benny Pond." The youth was in that numb grip of despair where men don't take the trouble to lie.

"What's your racket?"

"Musician, once."

There wasn't any need to throw a question beyond that. It was too apparent what the man was today. He was a deathly sick, whipped dog. Culver had hit upon a theory in the split seconds between the moment when he noticed the gun under the napkin and the moment when he dove for it. He hadn't changed that theory since. Now he cracked it, his hard, direct stare fixed on Benny Pond's pale face.

"Somebody hired you to shoot Menger," he said. "Probably fixed it for your family to get the money. Sold you the idea that you wouldn't live to take the rap. Right?"

Benny Pond stared sullenly at the table-top. He didn't attempt to answer.

Culver guessed again. "You've got a wife and kids, haven't you?"

The youth was startled. "Yes. Two girls. I—"

"Sure. They'd pick somebody like you. You fumbled your job. Now, your family won't get the money."

That shot went home. Benny Pond's luminous dark eyes bugged. "They—they got it. Before I tried to shoot—they didn't know, of course. But—"

He was frightened, breaking. Culver kept him on the run. "How much?"

"One thousand dollars."

Culver blinked. For one thousand dollars, this man had sold his last hours on earth, had whipped himself up to murdering a man whom he had never seen before—a thousand dollars that he would never touch himself. And some low heel of a human had trafficked pitilessly in the man's great need.

"They won't take it away from them—from my wife and kids?"

There was stark terror in the youth's face, terror beyond that which he had shown when he held the gun on Monk Menger.

Culver evaded the question. "Come clean, and I'll see what I can do about it. What was the proposition?"

It came tumbling out then. Benny Pond had been down and out and dying on his feet, faced with the certainty of leaving his family in poverty when he went. And one of the slimy rats who prey upon labor-unions, and know too much about labor business, had made a date for him "with a man who could help him out." Benny Pond hadn't known the man's name, but the fellow had given him a gun and a thousand dollars in an envelope for his family, and told him that he'd be better off in a prison hospital than walking around.

"He—he told me it would be tough on my family if I double-crossed him. I—I tried—"

"Sure, kid." Culver stood up. It was the way he had figured the play, and it was a dirty business. "I'll see you through, if you play my way and follow instructions. You're going to see the guy that hired you and you're going to tell him that you did the job, see?"

"But, I don't know—"

"That's all right. You're going to the Twin Moons. I'll tell you who to ask for. When he comes out, if he's the right one, you just walk up to him and tell him that you did the job. That's all."

"But—"

"Sure—you didn't do the job. I know that. What's a white lie between friends? You're going to play ball."

Benny Pond swallowed hard. "Yes—yes, sir," he said.

**AT THE** Twin Moons, Culver let the youth go in alone. He slipped in quietly himself and stood near the telephone switchboard. He watched Benny Pond send in the name by a haughty waiter—and he saw Sid Weyler come out.

Sid Weyler was short and had run to weight in the wrong places. He was flabby and his skin was dough-white, under any circumstances. It turned several shades whiter now when he saw Benny Pond. His normally pendulous lower lip dropped farther. He took a backward step, then reconsidered and came forward to face the music. In his swiftly shifting eyes there was written a war of resolves.

He wanted to disclaim all knowledge of Benny Pond, and yet he did not want to risk raised voices nor to call attention to himself by the type of argument that a frail, excitable invalid like Benny might be expected to stage.

Culver lounged by the switchboard. He was absorbed in the drama before him, and he didn't see the second invalid until too late. A tall, thin wreck of a man in an ill-fitting dinner-jacket rose jerkily from one of the easy-chairs in the reception-hall—and he had a gun in his hand when he rose. On his face, was the same desperate, hopeless resolve that had been on the face of Benny Pond.

Culver went for him lunging—but the gun cracked three times while he was crossing the reception-hall.

An Italian waiter just inside the dining-room door gave a loud shriek and dropped a dish-loaded tray. Sid Weyler clutched the gleaming-white shirt-front that was turning red with his blood, and his breath gurgled in his throat. He was folding forward when Culver brought his killer down.

The man was fighting like a wildcat. He was flailing with the gun and threshing around under Culver's grip. Culver missed two grabs for the gun, and then Sergeant Driscoll was in the picture with Dollar Hanlon at his heels. Driscoll twisted the gun away and the man went limp, his eyes desperate, defiant. Culver was breathing heavily.

"You can sweat the truth out of this guy, Sarge," he said. "Monk Menger hired him. It was Menger's out. Menger wouldn't have to kill a man who was dead already. This guy would keep buttoned up—but he probably got a grand for it. Tell him you'll take the dough away from his family if he doesn't come clean."

The expression on the thin man's face was enough to confirm Culver's guess, but he didn't want to look at the man's face. It was tough business. He turned away.

"Strange how the minds of two heels will work exactly the same way when they've been partners," he murmured. "Figure the odds against two men hitting on the same scheme at the same time!"

There was excitement at the door of the dining-room. Culver took the few seconds that he had in the clear to cross to the cowering Benny Pond. "Beat it, kid," he said. "Nobody knows you got that money now. Go to Arizona with it. It's better than a hospital in the gow."

He didn't wait to see him start. Dollar Hanlon was in the group around a sputtering, half-hysterical Italian waiter whose tray was on the floor with a bullet-hole in it and who was loudly exhibiting a hand that had been bullet-grazed. Sid Weyler's face had already been covered by a handkerchief by a doctor-guest. Dollar Hanlon saw Culver and his brows pulled down to a scowl.

"A swell job, you did. A shooting in my place."

"Sure." Culver shrugged. "But at the door of the dining-room, old settler. No damage in that. It advertises you." He waved to the waiter who was still carrying on noisily about his hand. "If that guy doesn't recover, you can have him stuffed, and attract tourists with him."

He turned on his heel. The flash-lead of the *Blue Barrel* for the morning-edition was already shaping in his brain—

> Look for the strangest defense in local criminal history in the trial of the man who sold his last hours on earth for one grand. And chalk up a believe-it-or-not. There would have been two murders, and two men with the same freak defense, if it weren't for a fellow named "Jones-My-Frand."

Elsewhere in the column, he'd have to work in a prediction that almost any jury would vote the hot-seat to Monk Menger who did his murder by proxy. The bet was a cinch.

# RING AROUND A MURDER

WHEN BOXING COMMISSIONER
HAGGERTY LEAPED FROM THE
TWELFTH FLOOR OF HIS HOTEL,
CULVER REFUSED TO BELIEVE THE
GRAND OLD MAN HAD DUTCHED IT.
BUT THE SOLE WITNESS TO THE
TRAGEDY WAS AS CROOKED AS
HAGGERTY HAD BEEN HONEST—
AND HE HAD TO BE THE ONE WHO
HELD CARDS THAT WOULD PROVE
MURDER KILLS BUT DOES NOT DIE.

**M**IKE HAGGERTY, the old gray lion of the boxing commission, was lying on the pavement with someone's coat thrown over him, and a morbidly curious crowd about him. He had crashed to the pavement from the twelfth floor of the Picardy Hotel, and a medical examination was sheer red tape.

Dean Culver stood on the edge of the crowd, his hands rammed into his pockets. He hadn't seen the body and didn't want to see it. He had been on his way to the Twin Moons to take over his evening trick as croupier behind the roulette wheel, when he'd seen the crowd. Somebody said that the body under the coat was Mike Haggerty, and Culver had stopped. He had always admired Mike Haggerty and believed in the things for which Haggerty stood.

There was a break in the crowd. Rex Krawley, the big bet-a-million man, was pushing through. He had the arm of Sergeant Driscoll of the homicide squad, and was talking for the world to hear.

"I tell you the *Blue Barrel* murdered Haggerty, Driscoll!" he said. "It was that item of his tonight. Mike blew up. I never saw him so upset. He just walked up and down and raved about it. He couldn't stand any cracks about crooked fights in this state, Driscoll. When he got all worked up—"

Rex Krawley choked a little, and waved his hand. "He just whirled around, took two steps and went right out the window. Something in his brain must have snapped—like that."

Krawley snapped his fingers. He was a heavy man, run to paunch but still solid across the chest and shoulders—a heavy-lidded man with the gambler's trick of keeping secrets out of his eyes. Culver was watching him grimly, his own eyes steady and no more revealing than Krawley's. He was suddenly conscious of someone beside him, and looked around.

"Harya, Scheckard?" he grunted. "Where do you come in on this?"

"I don't." Pat Scheckard was a precinct dick in a precinct where there were many protected gambling-houses and kindred establishments. He was a lean, hard man with the battered features of a pug, the eye of a cynic and a tired smile. He waved a hand at the coat-protected body.

"You think he dutched?"

"No. I don't." Culver's tone was emphatic. Scheckard nodded. He and Culver had always been friendly, but it was one of those spots where a copper doesn't commit himself even to friends.

"Hanging it on the *Blue Barrel* is rich," he said. "Pretty safe, too. Nobody knows who the *Blue Barrel* is—not even the paper that prints his stuff. They can hang anything on him. There isn't a rat, chiseler or hood in this town that wouldn't like to pour lead into the guy. Blaming Mike Haggerty on him doesn't make it any worse."

The precinct dick spat in the street. He was a square cop running under wraps. He flattened a night edition of the *Morning Star* against his thigh.

"This here is the item that Fatty is belching about," he said.

He ran a thick forefinger across the sports page, and brought it to rest against a boxed item that was headed by a cut of a smoking automatic pistol and the line *Blue Barrel.* There were such boxed items scattered all through the paper, and, wherever they appeared, the public knew that the publicity pistol was being leveled at another crook, chiseler or double-crosser. What Winchell was to Broadway, the *Blue Barrel* was to the world of great and petty crime. He was the unknown tipster who kept ahead of the headlines. Culver gravely read the item under Scheckard's finger—

> Another old favorite is due to punch the comeback leather at startling odds. The details have all been arranged, but a rush of sucker money can change the scenario. Lay off betting on comeback fights.

Scheckard was looking thoughtfully at the corpse. "Any sap would get what that item meant," he said. "It's in the bag for Dusty Hodge to knock out Steve Nixon. Fights have been on the square since Haggerty's been commissioner. The old man would feel pretty bad—"

The gong of the dead wagon sounded up the street. Culver shrugged slightly. "Mad—not bad, Scheckard," he said.

"Sure." Scheckard grinned his weary grin. "But the verdict will still be suicide. Nobody will even mention that Slag Jensen, Hodge's manager, was in the apartment and took a run-out powder after the old man went out the window."

Culver stiffened. "Was he?"

Scheckard met his eyes. "Maybe I've been listenin' to gossip."

"Maybe. Thanks, Scheck."

CULVER TURNED and started down the block. That was his way of saying good-night. Scheckard had given him a tip, because Scheckard liked him and had liked the old man. He couldn't use that tip in any way that would embarrass Scheckard, and the dick knew that he wouldn't. Culver's mouth was a straight line.

He was headed again for the Twin Moons. There was something to think about in the fact that Haggerty had been closeted with Krawley, the odds-layer, and Jensen, manager of the comeback slugger, just after the *Blue Barrel* item hit the street—something to think about in the fact that Haggerty had come out of that conference dead, and that Jensen had run away. Rex Krawley had elected to face the music and admit that he had been in the room with Haggerty. But Krawley also had enough influence to put his story over.

"And Krawley thought he was big enough to hang Haggerty's death on the *Blue Barrel*," Culver muttered.

His jaw was hard. The Twin Moons was only a half block down from the Picardy, but Culver had to elbow his way through the denizens of the district, lured into the open by the shock of violent tragedy—hard-eyed men, greasy men, and men who couldn't even stand still without suggesting a furtive crouch. Once clear of the pressing crowd, he had to pass doorways out of which ratty faces peered. He smiled grimly.

He was walking down a rotten block, and he would spend the night behind a roulette wheel under the lights in a popular gambling-spot. A hundred pairs of eyes would pass over him heedlessly—eyes that could be hardened into hatred by a whisper.

He was walking away from possible death, past possible death and into possible death.

Dean Culver was the *Blue Barrel*.

**IT WASN'T** yet eleven o'clock. The Twin Moons had a fair crowd, but mostly regulars—the players who play through the theater hours and drift home about midnight. Culver, who wasn't slated to take over the wheel until eleven-thirty, looked in at the big room.

Phil Ordway, one of the regular players of Culver's wheel, was cashing in early. He had an enormous stack of chips, and, as usual, when that happened, he was drunk. He had always had drunkard's luck.

"The only kind of luck that he ever did have, poor devil." Culver shook his head.

He liked Ordway. The man had been one of the greatest big-league shortstops of all time until he became mixed up in a game-throwing scandal and was barred from organized baseball for life—barred despite his sworn protest that gamblers had framed him to cover up some crook who had played ball with them.

Ordway was a little man, and rolling across the big room now with a fixed and cheerful grin on his wizened, leathery face. Swagger Brice was behind him—an overdressed hood who did Krawley's errands for him. Culver's eyes ranged the room.

Slag Jensen, the tall, sad-faced manager of Dusty Hodge, was watching the play at the wheel. He didn't look like a man who had run out of a room from which another man had plunged to death, but he wasn't supposed to look like that. The Twin Moons would probably be his alibi, and the memories of even honest people are tricky. There would be people there who would swear that he'd been in the room all night. Culver turned away.

The man lay on his back, heavy pick-point in his skull.

He crossed to the sound-proof, insulated phone booths that were the last word in gambling-house accessories. He didn't usually use a phone in any place where he was known. Tonight was different. He called the *Morning Star,* and, when he got Randall, the city editor, on the line, his voice deepened.

"Randall? *Blue Barrel* speaking. Catch this for a first-page box. 'The man who kept boxing honest in this state did not take a dive.'"

He heard the city editor's low whistle. "Will you be able to protect that crack after you make it, *B.B.?*"

"Take bets on it."

Culver hung up with a snap, and left the booth. He was a slender, wiry, inconspicuous man in a dark suit. Standing there outside of the booth, he looked like what he was supposed to be—the croupier of the Twin Moons whom thousands saw, and few remembered. Inside of him there burned a hot fire.

He was on his own in a murder case. The homicide squad would never get the case to solve, because the coroner's jury would call it suicide. Who was going to buck the word of a big shot like Krawley when he gave his account of what supposedly occurred while he was alone in a room with a man who could never contradict him?

**THERE WAS** an argument taking place on the other side of the foyer. Phil Ordway was shaking a rolled copy of the *Morning Star* under Swagger Brice's nose.

"The *Blue Barrel* says so, and that's enough for me," he said. "The fight's in the bag. Dusty Hodge is going to knock Nixon out. I won a lot of money here tonight. I'm going to bet it that way."

"Aw, you're crazy!" Swagger Brice was sneering at him. "Hodge couldn't even hit Nixon the best day he ever saw, and he's all red with rust now."

"Nixon will take a dive to him."

"Baloney. The *Blue Barrel* doesn't even dare say that. There's libel laws. He words his stuff up funny so it reads two ways, and he always comes out right."

"He says it straight enough for me," said Ordway. "I'm betting. It's in the bag. You gamblers want to hog all of the short end. Well, I like to take falls out of gamblers. They owe me a lot. I'm betting Hodge."

"Someday the *Blue Barrel* is going to end up on his face, and you'll have to do your own thinking." Brice was still sneering.

Culver turned and went down the line to Dollar Hanlon's office. He had to report that he would be late taking over the wheel tonight. He didn't say why—he didn't have to say why with Hanlon. Culver came out of the manager's office with narrowed eyes. He knew the chance he was taking tonight. For the first time in his double career of Dean Culver and the *Blue Barrel*, he was going to meet a tipster face to face. He had a date to meet the man who had given him the fatal Hodge-Nixon fight-tip down on the waterfront, but he didn't know who the man was.

Phil Ordway came reeling out of the men's room. His face brightened when he saw Culver. "Culver," he said thickly. "Jus' the man I want to see. Wait up, will ya?"

Culver slowed and the former big-leaguer gripped his lapel. "Come in here a minute." Culver accompanied him reluctantly back to the men's room.

Ordway was taking an opal ring from his finger. "I'm drunk, Culver. Always get in trouble when I'm drunk.

Never want to lose my ring. Take care of it for me." He was pressing the ring on Culver.

Culver frowned. He knew the story of that opal. It was one of two that had been in the ear-rings of Phil Ordway's wife. Doris Ordway had died of shock when Ordway was busted out of the big leagues as a crook. Phil Ordway had the ear-rings as finger-rings now. One he wore on his finger, and one—as very few people knew—he carried under his shirt on a cord that hung around his neck. When he was drunk, he always appointed someone to take care of the one ring. Culver turned the ring over in his hand.

Ordway was passing a big roll of currency after the ring. Culver shook his head. "Get Hanlon to put them in the safe for you, Phil," he said.

Ordway's face lost its good nature. "Nix to that. I don't trust any gambler. I hate them all, see?"

"What do you think I am?" Culver smiled.

"You're a square guy who works for a gambler. There's a difference, see?"

"O.K." Culver slipped the ring on his own finger, and tucked the bills away in his pocket.

Ordway still clung to him. "You're taking care of them personal, now. No turning 'em over to any safe. Promise?"

"Check."

Culver shook hands with him gravely, and went out. There was usually very little percentage in arguing with drunks, and Ordway was the kind of a man that a fellow did favors for. Culver was shaking his head, however.

"It would have to be tonight," he said.

He was thinking of the dark rendezvous ahead of him, and his fingers moved instinctively to the automatic under his armpit. There were occasions when he needed more than a gun at a column-head.

As he was leaving the Twin Moons, Rex Krawley came in. The mask of tragedy, that the man had worn for the cops, had been wiped from his fat features, and there was something offensively complacent about him. He knew Culver, but he didn't speak. He didn't figure that there was anything that Culver could do for him. He was the kind of man who doesn't even spend a nod where it doesn't figure to bring returns.

**THE WATERFRONT** was darker than a Negro's pocket. The sound of the river was a sighing swish out of the blackness. It was the zero hour when nobody was at work, and when the nocturnal prowlers were not yet about. Dean Culver sat on a box at the midway point of a long pier and kept his eyes on the broad sweep of levee that the spot commanded. He could see the mouths of four streets that flowed into Levee Street, and he was not conspicuous himself. There were low-power street lamps on those streets, and he was in comparative darkness.

"You carry a pickax. If I like your looks, I'll follow you until I'm sure that you're alone. Nope—you've got to be the lad who takes the chances. I've got no reasons for popping you off. Maybe you've got some reasons for plugging me."

Culver went slowly over his instructions to the unknown tipster. He remembered them, word for word, and they checked. The tipster had shown good faith, in the first place, by leaving a number for the *Blue Barrel* to call. The man had taken a chance there, and Culver had played fair. He hadn't located the phone and descended upon it in person.

"He had some strong reason for tipping me, as well as something else to tell me."

Culver was feeling tense. The river and the levee seemed unnaturally quiet. Slight sounds carried for long distances, and he had the idea that any sudden sound of real volume would be too much for human nerves to stand.

One reeling drunk passed along Levee Street, and one furtive figure that walked with head low—but neither was a man with a pickax. Culver's uneasiness increased. The *Blue Barrel* was a badly wanted individual in many quarters, and a complicated set-up for snaring him would be justified by the results. This could be a trap, and, if it were, he would have to move fast when it was sprung.

He still thought that the pickax identification had been an inspiration. No one was likely to be carrying a pickax along the levee at night except the man who would use it as identification. Yet, to strangers, the sight of a man with a pickax in this neighborhood would arouse no curiosity.

"Fifteen minutes late." Culver consulted his watch.

He was dressed in a dark business suit in contrast to the dinner clothes that he wore at the Twin Moons. He had his coat collar turned up, his sweeping hat brim snapped down. Ordway's opal was on his finger, Ordway's cash in his pocket.

He was increasingly conscious of the cash and the opal, as the minutes went by. He had responsibilities enough of his own, without carrying responsibility for another man. He swore softly, and ached for a cigarette. He could work all night in the Twin Moons and never break in the rhythm of collecting and paying bets, without being conscious that he had nerves at all. He could escort heavy winners home from the place with their cash and be as cold as an iceberg despite the ever-to-be-reckoned possibility of gun-toting hoods. Sitting here in the darkness was something else. It threw him too much back upon himself.

He had been framed once and knew the inside of a big penitentiary from firsthand experience. He had been a police reporter in Chicago, and the underworld had made him the goat of a monstrous frame at a time when the memory of the Lingle case was still fresh, and when an accused reporter didn't have a chance. He came out of the pen bitter and suspicious. He'd been paying the underworld back ever since, shooting hard and straight with the *Blue Barrel*. But he'd never escaped the fear of a frame, the tendency in his own mind to magnify the appearance of things and to look for conspiracies.

He scented a trap now, and was no longer content to wait for the unknown tipster. He looked at his watch again. The man was twenty-two minutes overdue, and that was too long. Culver had the most dangerous part of his adventure ahead of him. He had to leave the place of rendezvous.

The tipster, of course, had not known where Culver was to wait. He had known only that he must walk along the levee carrying a pick, and that Culver would see him. If the man were crooked, however, he would know that tonight the *Blue Barrel* was waiting somewhere along Levee Street. Sharp eyes might be on watch, and nervous fingers hover on triggers.

**CULVER MOVED** slowly down the pier, staying in the shadows. He had fast, educated hands and a gun under his armpit. He had eyes sharpened by hour after hour of watching the spinning ball and the numbers that won or lost.

Levee Street remained quiet. He reached the end of the pier, crossed the street and moved along the building fronts. He saw a drunk sitting on the curb, but the man did not raise his head. There was another man, in a tattered shirt and trousers of soiled duck, who slept on a stoop. No one was in motion, and nothing menacing moved in the darkness.

He moved toward the bridge five blocks away. He would turn left there and proceed up town. He was puzzled at the silence and the absence of any frame-up evidence. If the tipster had been on the level, then why hadn't he shown up?

He passed two dimly lighted saloons. There was a sound of tin-pan music from within, but no one appeared outside. He was beyond the area that his spot on the pier had commanded. He stopped suddenly.

Almost at his feet lay the man with the pickax.

Someone had wielded that pickax with deadly effect. The man lay on his back, with his arms outspread, the point of the heavy pick buried in his skull. Around his head, there was a pool of blood that had spread in an even circle. One leg was doubled up under his body. He had fallen as if struck down in mid-leap while striving to escape from the fate that eventually overtook him.

Culver swore softly, and bent low. He was fully aware of the target that he made, but he was not going to get it going away as this poor unfortunate wretch had got it. If the man with the pick had died because he had a date with the *Blue Barrel,* then there might be gunmen hanging around. But the immediate area around the body was within Culver's vision, and a hidden gunman would have to shoot from fairly long range into darkness. Culver was ready to risk being able to return fire.

He was down on one knee, careful to avoid the pool of blood. It was too dark to observe details, and he didn't intend to light a match. The left side of the man's face was against the pavement, the right side up. Culver whistled softly.

The dead man was Phil Ordway.

The night was so quiet that the darkness seemed to tick. Culver crouched there above the dead body, and his thoughts raced. There was the identifying pickax, and there was Phil Ordway. Out of the grim facts, emerged two alternatives. Ordway had followed the man who was to meet the *Blue Barrel* and had been killed for his curiosity, or Ordway was the mysterious tipster.

"Phil wasn't the shadowing type."

Culver whispered the words. He was wishing that he had known that Ordway was the tipster. It would have helped. He could see a lot of things plainly now. Ordway had been no more drunk at the Twin Moons than Culver himself. He had been putting on an act that would enable him to shake anyone who might be curious about his movements, preparing an explanation if he should be seen with so ridiculous a thing as a pick. No one in the city hated gamblers more sincerely, nor with greater cause. It was easy to believe that Ordway would play with the *Blue Barrel*, if he hoped to strike a blow at the gamblers who were preparing a fixed fight.

The killing of Mike Haggerty had come first. After that had come the killing of Ordway himself.

Culver rose slowly. It would be sloppy thinking to say that Ordway had been killed because he had a date with the *Blue Barrel*. His murderers hadn't known that or they would have staged their killing differently—would have included the *Blue Barrel* in the slaughter.

"He was killed because he had money and he was going to bet that money on Hodge and help to bust the odds."

Culver was reconstructing the picture of the elegant Swagger Brice who stuck to Phil Ordway like a leech at the Twin Moons. Swagger Brice dressed well because he killed at high pay and threatened death at high pay. Culver's lips were tight.

He bent again above the body and searched it carefully. There was a creased line across his forehead, when he got through. Someone had searched Ordway before him, and thus far the scenario clicked—but what next? He had the glimmer of a plan.

He had to make a move either as Dean Culver or as the *Blue Barrel*. It was his show. The death of Mike Haggerty had been laid at his door. The man who had been his tipster was murdered, possibly because Culver had made the date in a spot where murder was easily staged.

**ORDWAY'S OPAL** ring was still on his finger. He turned it around thoughtfully. There was an idea in it, just as there was danger in having Ordway's ring and Ordway's money in his possession while he stood above Ordway's looted corpse.

Down Levee Street someone was whistling *Annie Laurie.*

He saw the whistler—a fat harness bull whose badge caught the dim light and threw it back in a silvery flash.

"That bull rates an item. So afraid he'll walk into trouble that he whistles as he walks!"

He waited there and listened to the strains of *Annie Laurie* becoming louder and more distinct, as the musical, and unsuspecting, cop walked on to his date with death in the dark.

For the first time since he reached the levee, his attention was concentrated on a single object, and, for the moment, he forgot that the buildings were divided by area-ways. A low, gruff voice reminded him too late.

"Step in here, mugg, and keep your hands up!" it said.

Culver's body stiffened, and he swore under his breath. He'd been playing the fringes too long not to know the tone of a man with a gun. He'd also been playing those fringes long enough to play quiet when the voice with the drop spoke. His hands went up reluctantly, and he backed into the areaway.

"If it's a stick-up, the mugg will have rich pickings," he thought. "But I don't think it's a stick-up."

The gun met his spine at the mouth of the areaway, and he kept backing.

"Honest citizen, ain't you?" the man behind the gun chuckled. "Stumble right onto a corpse and scatter, as soon as you see a cop coming."

"You didn't rush out with any identification yourself." Culver's voice was a low growl.

He wasn't kidding himself that the presence of the cop within a block would deter the man behind him from pressing the trigger, if he made a play. The kind of stick-up men who step out of areaways, usually know where their areaways lead. This mugg could shoot and be blocks away before pursuit got going, and Culver wouldn't count much, personally, on a cop who whistled his way around a dark beat.

"Hold it. Let me get a look at you."

They had rounded an L-bend in the areaway, and the man with the gun flipped the switch on his pocket flash suddenly. There was a pale cone of light that hit the back of Culver's neck and steadied.

"Turn around!"

He turned and met the light with his jaw squared. The man behind the light swore softly, then chuckled.

"Culver," he said. "Now fancy meeting you like this!" The chuckle died out of his voice, even as he spoke. There was suspicion in the tone, reserve.

Culver could feel the tension that built up in the man, after the first startled second of recognition. As his own eyes became accustomed to the glare, he could look through and beyond it to the fancy cut of a blue suit, the brightly colored shirt and the gaudy tie of Swagger Brice.

"I've got a job to do," Culver growled back. "Now, where do you rate?"

"What job?" Brice was standing very close, and he had the gun held against Culver's body just above the belt. There was a glitter in his eyes, a rasp to his voice, that spelled shaky nerves and made him as dangerous with a gun as a hophead.

"The Twin Moons sees the heavy winners home with their dough, Brice." Culver kept his voice level, indifferent. "Ordway wouldn't take an escort, so I tailed him. I lost him a while, then—" He shrugged.

"Yeah? Well, you're a liar, see? He left his dough there. He didn't have a dime."

OUT ON the street, there was a sudden shrill blast of a police whistle and the bang of a cop's nightstick against the pavement. The gay whistler of *Annie Laurie* had found the corpse. Swagger Brice crouched a little, the gun still held hard.

"Nerts," he said. "I should barber the night away with you! I got a car. Get moving, and walk soft."

He took a slithering sidestep that put him around Culver, the gun still held level. Culver shrugged, moved forward. Mentally, he was way ahead of Brice. But he couldn't see where it did him much good, as long as the fancy hood kept the physical advantage.

He knew, for instance, what was still a hazy idea in the brain of Swagger Brice. Swagger had given up on the job of trying to decide what to do with him. Swagger would take him to someone better qualified to make decisions than he was himself. Eventually, Swagger, or someone else, would recognize what a blunder Swagger had pulled when he stated so vehemently that Phil Ordway had had no money on him.

The car was in the alleyway—a dark, inconspicuous roadster of a common make. Brice still played top dog with the gun. "You drive," he said. "Do it like I tell you to do it, see? Just don't get ideas."

"Oke. Maybe you know what you are doing." Culver still acted bored. It was the best way of keeping Swagger Brice jabbed off balance and unable to make up his mind. Antagonism would only stimulate a man like Brice.

Culver slid under the wheel. "Where to?"

"Just drive out. Keep the speed down and roll uptown. I'll say 'when.'"

The car came to life, and Culver drove. He heard the cop's whistle answered, then the beat of other nightsticks against pavement. There would be prowl-cars on the move, too, but he tooled the roadster out of the alley and headed it uptown at a sedate speed without figuring prowl-car cops into his scenario. There was a certain routine bent to a copper's mind that would take him to the scene of an alarm with scant attention for innocent-looking cars that seemed to be minding their own business.

"The Normandie. Take it out there."

Swagger Brice was slumped in the cushion beside Culver. His gun wasn't in evidence, but there was gun in his voice. Culver nodded and turned the wheel. The Normandie was three blocks from the Twin Moons—a flash apartment house that had been built with honest money, wrecked by a crooked receivership and used now as a headquarters for chiselers, bums and people who lived by their alleged wits. Things happened at the Normandie that would make headlines if they reached the men who wrote headlines. But unless the guns barked too loud or the action became too raw, no one at the Normandie ever became curious.

"Walk in friendly and natural, or I'll dump you on the pavement." Brice talked out of the side of his mouth, as Culver brought the car to the curb in the space marked off as *Hotel Entrance*.

Culver nodded again and got out. He had no intention of making a play. There was no percentage in it.

He was very conscious, however, of the opal ring on his finger and the money in his pocket, as he entered the elevator ahead of Swagger Brice. He was wondering who was upstairs, and just how sharp the brains were that would mull over the evidence that Brice brought in, also if anyone would connect up Phil Ordway's hatred of gamblers, the *Blue Barrel's* tip-off, and Culver's presence on the levee where Ordway died. A skilful connecting of those facts would spell *Blue Barrel,* and Culver wondered.

**THERE WERE** only two men in the tenth-floor apartment. Rex Krawley was sitting in a big easy-chair with his coat off, his sweat-wet shirt clinging to the outlines of his broad chest and folding damply over the roll of fat around his middle. Slag Jensen, the manager of Dusty Hodge, was in another chair across the room, the only Scandinavian fight manager in the business—a tall, powerful, gray-faced man with battered features.

Swagger Brice became suddenly quite self-possessed. "I gotta see you alone for a minute, boss," he said. "Better tell Slag to watch that Culver cookie close. I'll tell you about him."

Rex Krawley had a reputation for being able to see through concrete. He took one look at Brice, and heaved himself to his feet. "How about this Culver's gun? You got one, Culver?"

"Sure." Culver drew it from the shoulder holster, acutely conscious of the sudden stiffening in Swagger Brice. He presented it, butt first, to Krawley.

The big man took it and dropped it carelessly in his side pocket. "See has he got another one, Brice!" he grunted. Culver held his hands out from his sides, and Brice slapped him over.

"He's clean," he said.

"O.K. Let's hear what you got to say. Watch that guy, Jensen. You, Culver, keep your nose clean!"

Krawley was casual, offhand, very much the boss. Culver watched him go into the next room with Brice, then looked across at Jensen. He was not forgetting that it was Slag Jensen who had dusted out of the picture after Mike Haggerty hit the pavement, nor that Slag Jensen was the manager of a comeback fighter who figured to win a fixed fight for the gambling ring.

Jensen was watching him, grim suspicion in his eyes. There were sheds of battered gristle protruding over those eyes of Jensen's, and shapeless lumps over his cheekbones that spoke of days when Jensen was doing the fighting himself instead of the managing. It was hard to guess at what he might have looked like if he hadn't been punched around. Now, he looked definitely and uncompromisingly hard.

"You sit right there," he said. He had one fist doubled up. It was bigger than two ordinary fists.

"They took my gun away," Culver laughed. "I'm not going to bang you out of the picture before you get a chance to yell for help."

He was on his feet, crossing the room. Jensen started up from his chair. Culver didn't break stride. "You take life too seriously," he said. "I just want a light for a cigarette—"

He had the cigarette case half out of his pocket, and was stretching his hand out to Jensen for a match, when he tripped over the footstool that Jensen had been using before he started to rise. Culver cursed convincingly, as he took a header hard. The cigarette case bounced to the rug, and Culver made a clumsy grab at Jensen for support. The big Scandinavian was off balance, and went back into the chair in a sprawl.

"Sorry!" Culver fought for balance. It had been quick work, but he had transferred Ordway's stuff into Jensen's pocket.

Culver was lighting one of the matches when Krawley came back with Swagger Brice. Jensen still looked puzzled. Krawley's fat face was viciously hostile.

"Culver, you're going to come clean with me. What were you doing on Levee Street?"

"Watching Brice kill Ordway with a pick."

"You're a liar!"

"Phil Ordway talked big, and he talked loud, and, when he had money, he bet it." Culver shrugged. "If he didn't have a big wad to bet, his talk wouldn't make much difference. With the wad, he'd get other bettors to follow his example and bet on Hodge. That would blow hell out of

your betting-coup. You have to bet against the suckers—
not with them."

**THE ROOM** was deadly quiet. Swagger Brice had
slipped into a crouch. Rex Krawley had his big body drawn
straight. "So what?"

"So Brice draws the job of getting Ordway's wad," said
Culver. "He follows him, and he doesn't figure out the
pickax play, but he tries the stick-up, anyway. Ordway's got
guts enough to fight it out with a pickax but he hasn't got
strength enough."

Culver was reconstructing what could have, and must
have happened. He was watching his men. Brice's face told
him that he had hit it on the head.

He whirled suddenly toward Jensen.

"You're a sucker," Culver growled. "When Haggerty
called you and Krawley up to his room about that phony
fight of yours, and Krawley lost his head, you let him make
a goat out of you. Krawley knocks the old man out the
window but you're the one who takes a run-out. What did
Krawley tell you? Did he tell you that he'd be brave and
face the music alone because he had influence? Sure. It gave
him an out to have somebody run away from the scene,
you sap!"

Krawley was big and heavy, but he had the deceptive
speed of a grizzly bear. Culver had just a flash of the man
bearing down on him, and then a heavy right hand caught
him and slapped him down.

Like something glimpsed dimly through a fog, he saw
Swagger Brice start his draw, saw Krawley swaying above
him and Jensen half out of the chair.

It was a bad spot, but there was only one thing to do with
it—bore in. Eyes narrowed on Krawley, Culver came erect.

"Yes, in a pinch, you'd call a copper. You threatened to call them on me. Before I came in, you had Jensen greased for the Ordway slaughter to get rid of him."

His voice was lashing fury, and that last statement staggered even the invincible Krawley. The moment of surprise was all Culver needed. He held out his hand.

"Look at that ring, Jensen. Ordway had me keep it for him. You've heard about that ring. Everyone has. Most people knew that it had a mate that Ordway wore on a string." His jaw was hard, jutting. "Ordway had a roll of bills, too, Jensen. Look in your pocket, if you don't think you were being framed."

He hurled the words too fast and too hard to be stopped by surprised men. Jensen's big hand dipped into his pocket and came out fast. A roll of bills and an opal ring spilled on the floor, and Jensen's curses spilled out with them.

The big man was across the room in a flailing charge, his face a study in dull rage. He didn't have a gun, but Rex Krawley didn't have a chance to use the one that he had, either. The Scandinavian's big fist caught him, as he dipped for the draw, and there was another fist coming.

Swagger Brice had his gun halfway out of its holster, when Culver hit him. Culver was swinging fast without waiting to get set, and Brice staggered sidewise under the blow. He fired blindly.

There was a hoarse bellow, and a grunt from across the room—then Culver was on top of Swagger Brice, his fists pumping. Swagger tried to use the gun, and it cost him the precious second that would have protected his chin. Culver felt the shock run up his arm, as his knuckles banged to the button. Then Brice was plunging forward on his face, and Culver had the gun.

Culver turned like a cat. He had the gun poised for action, but there was no action. Rex Krawley was lying on his face. Jensen was sitting, his hand holding a jaw that gushed red.

"Went right through him. Hit me—"

**CULVER BENT** hurriedly over Rex Krawley. The man was breathing heavily, and his eyelids were fluttering, but there was strength in him. Someone was pounding at the door, and, even if this was the Normandie, the party had been exceptionally noisy. Culver let them hammer and picked up the direct-connected outside phone. He called the precinct station house and kept his eye, and the gun, on the fast-recovering Brice.

"Scheckard?" he said into the phone. "Listen, Pat. This is Culver. I got something big that I'll hand you on a platter, if you ease me out of it, O.K.?—"

# ABOUT THE AUTHOR

**I** **VENTED** my first squawk at life in the City of New
York on November 16, 1900, and managed to weather
the hazards of Manhattan boyhood until I was sixteen;
then, while the native New Yorkers of my age were pouring in from Kansas, Missouri and Minnesota, I followed
the family star of destiny to Colorado. I had prepared at
Manhattan College of New York for an engineering career,
but this proved to be a misdeal and I took a whirl at reporting on a Denver daily. I never progressed past the cub stage
and was fervently advised by a harassed city editor that I
never would. After that I became one of the young men
who signed the coupon.

I went to work for a power company and studied engineering some more at night. Then a publicity job for a big
electrical manufacturer took me all over the West and for
a while I was national publicity director for Station KFKX
at Hastings, Nebraska, the first rebroadcasting station in
the world. About this time, somebody told me about the
easy work and big pay of fictioneers and I decided to try
my hand. By the time I found out how badly I had been
deceived I was too badly bitten by the bug to ever escape.

I stayed with publicity work till February 1, 1929, but
fiction was a side line for years. Since then, it has been the
whole works. Now I toil not, neither do I spin—all in the

world that I have to do is bite my nails and fight a type-writer and think up enough ideas to keep the wolf from having whelps on the Barrett door-step. An easy life if you like your ease to come in packages that are so hard to open.

My most interesting experience was an assignment to write an advertising campaign addressed to oil operators. This took me into all the leading oil fields in the United States and has supplied me with a wealth of story material. Another source has been aviation. I took up flying to get material and have been handling the publicity work of the Guardian Aircraft Corporation. Without taking very much time, it repaid me mightily in flying lore and experience.

Thus far, I have sold several hundred yarns and hope to sell many more. I've got to. I am married to the best little "encourager" in the world; an ink-slinger of no little skill herself. If I ever write love stories for *Argosy*, they'll be authentic, too, because—ah, well, why should you look in my lighted window. Two kiddies, boy and girl, complete the narrative—and that's all there is. Sorry if there is nothing exciting in this, but if the thing had a plot or any particular drama, I'd stick a name like Pete Jones on myself and sell the darn thing!

www.ingramcontent.com/pod-product-compliance
Lightning Source LLC
Chambersburg PA
CBHW020554020726
47494CB00006B/2067